SEARCHING FOR GRACE

Praise for *Caught in the Crossfire*

"Juliann Rich has written a coming of age story that is at once bittersweet, fun, and sexy, capturing the complex layers of angst and joy that teens encounter when caught between wanting to be accepted and being true to who they are."—Alex Sanchez, author of *Rainbow Boys* and *The God Box*

"*Caught In the Crossfire* speaks to those of us who know what it's like to search for ourselves, then turn away when we're not sure what we see. Jonathan's struggles go straight to your heart, and his decisions will have you both rooting for him and holding your breath."—Kirstin Cronn-Mills, author of *Beautiful Music For Ugly Children*, 2013 Lambda Literary Award finalist and 2014 ALA Stonewall Award winner

"Rich's beautifully written coming-out and coming-of-age story appeals to any reader who has stood at such crossroads." —Mary Carroll Moore, author of *Qualities of Light* and *Your Book Starts Here*

"An honest, heartbreaking, and beautiful story about first love, readers will immediately fall for golden boy, Jonathan, and, at the same time, be drawn to Ian's wild ways. The relationship that follows is sweet, awkward, frustrating, and downright steamy at times. You'll be rooting for them from the first chapter until the last."—Dawn Klehr, author of *The Cutting Room Floor*

"Caught between the need for a spiritual relationship and the desire for a human one, Jonathan must take a journey common to many LGBT teens and their families. If you thought gay teens discovering themselves didn't belong in the same pages with spirituality, think again. This much-needed story doesn't shy away from tough questions and tense scenes—but tackles them head-on with humor, sensuality, and hope."—Rachel Gold, author of *Being Emily*, Golden Crown Literary Award winner and 2013 Lambda Literary Award finalist

By the Author

Caught in the Crossfire

Searching for Grace

SEARCHING FOR GRACE

by

Juliann Rich

A Division of Bold Strokes Books

2014

SEARCHING FOR GRACE

ISBN 13: 978-1-62639-196-3

This Trade Paperback Original Is Published By
Bold Strokes Books, Inc.
P.O. Box 249
Valley Falls, NY 12185

First Edition: September 2014

Credits
Editors: Lynda Sandoval and Cindy Cresap
Production Design: Stacia Seaman
Cover Design by Sheri (graphicartist2020@hotmail.com)

DuBOIS

Acknowledgments

No book is the result of just one person's efforts. The following people have been instrumental in the writing and polishing of *Searching for Grace* and deserve more thanks than I can offer here:

Len Barot and all the hardworking folks at Bold Strokes Books. You've believed in *Searching for Grace* and guided me every step of the way.

Lynda Sandoval and Cindy Cresap, my editors. You've helped me take *Searching for Grace* to its highest potential and made the journey a blast to travel.

Saritza Hernández, my friend and agent. How blessed am I to walk this road with you!

Aren Sabers, Maggie Wimberley, and J. Leigh Bailey, my friends and fellow writers. *Searching for Grace* would not be the book it is without you.

The writing community at The Loft Literary Center and the fine folk at Mn Kidlit. You've taught me something every time I've gotten together with you (and not just about where to find the best brew in the Twin Cities!). It is an honor to be a part of your group.

Jeff, my husband extraordinaire. You are my grace. Matthias, my beautiful son. You are my inspiration. My incredible mom. You will always be my first and best teacher.

Thank you all.

For my husband, Jeff, who is my grace.

CHAPTER ONE

It's all a blur.

A blur of lights blinding me as I fly down the long hallway, feet first like I'm a kid again, shooting off the end of a slide. Is anyone going to catch me? The bed I'm lying on jerks to a stop, and I look for my mother in the blur of bodies that surround me like a white canvas. Even their expressions are stretched thin. A bit of teal seeps into view. Leans over me and flashes a light in my eyes. It burns all the way through my skull. HEY, THAT HURTS! I tell the bit of teal, and she stops, but a blotch of blue hovers in the background. Breaking the line of horizon.

Sketch, make him go away.

I can't focus.

I slip into the darkness.

Sounds blur too. I discover this as I float to the surface.

Beeping and humming, the sounds of machines. Whispers and footsteps, the sounds of people. *Head laceration approximately four inches long. Pupils dilated and uneven. Page neurology and psych for consult.*

The words and noises blur into a song I don't recognize or like. The tempo is too quick. *I can't dance to this,* I tell Ian, but he isn't here.

"What happened?" The blotch in blue barges into the

foreground. He leans over me, so close I can tell he ate onions recently.

"Sir, you need to wait outside," a voice from the canvas of white tells him.

"I don't think you understand. I need to ask that kid a few questions." Onion Breath fumes at White Canvas.

"I don't think you understand. Right now that kid is my patient, and my only concern is what he needs."

Stop calling me THAT KID! I try to sit up and shout at them.

"Two milligrams Versed STAT!" Something stabs me in the arm. A bitter taste floods my mouth. The ceiling swirls, and I forget what I was going to say. A flash of light burns my eyes. A voice bangs in my head. It's White Canvas.

"Can you tell me your name?"

Oh yeah, that's what I was going to tell them. "Jonathan. My name is Jonathan." My voice sounds weird, like I'm talking with a mouthful of marbles. I try again, but the weight is back, pulling me under.

"That's great, Jonathan. Do you know what day it is?"

"Friday," I mumble.

White Canvas chuckles.

"Right. How about the date? Do you know that?"

"October…something. Homecoming, I think."

"Good."

I can tell he's got more questions, but Onion Breath pushes past him and leans over me.

"Who did this to you, kid?"

"What are you talking about?" I ask.

His eyes narrow. "What kind of a game are you trying to play?" His face hovers inches above mine. I close my eyes and try to concentrate.

I'd answer him. Really, I would. Except it's all a blur.

Chapter Two

Drag and scissor!" The voice came from a moving streak of blue and white. Pete Mitchell, our center forward, was going fast. Too fast. Luke Williams, a new transfer from Minnetonka Public, charged down the soccer field and broke left, betting Pete would lose control of the ball. Pete's left foot swung out over the ball, snapped back, and kicked with the outside of his foot. A reverse scissor.

Sweet! The ball ricocheted right to where I stood, melting under the glare of the sun, ready to run with it.

"Nice pickup, Coop!" Pete shouted behind me. I glanced back and saw Luke kicking the ground. I breezed past Ethan Spencer. Danced around Zack Phillips and Austin Flaherty. They were good. Better than good, actually, but I knew their moves. Clear green stretched before me. Just the goal and me and Brandon Schultz between us. Blood rushed through my veins, feeding the tensed leg muscles that drove me forward.

"Bring it home, Coop!" Pete shouted behind me. Brandon danced in the net, his muscles twitching in anticipation. I charged down the center, forcing him to run forward. Forcing him to guess which way I'd break. I let my body weight shift to the right. Selling it. It was subtle, but the best feints usually are. Brandon bought it. He charged to my right, leaving the left side of the net wide open. I didn't have to look to know that triumph was written across Pete's face.

The warning in my right ankle came two seconds too late. It wasn't ready. Wasn't fully healed. Couldn't take the pressure.

My ankle buckled.

I lurched sideways, my arms flailing through the air to grab for something. Anything. The ground rushed me. A flash of green and then my right shoulder slammed into the hard turf.

Brandon broke left. He passed the ball to Ethan, who laughed and ran with it.

"Mother Hubbard!" I swore, facedown on the field, as the game played around me in the ninety-degree late August heat.

"Circle up, guys," Coach Thomas called out after the scrimmage. I wiped the sweat from my forehead and fell in place with my team.

"First, you all right, Jonathan?"

"Fine. I just lost my balance for a second."

"That's all it takes for this game to turn," Coach said.

I swallowed and shifted my weight.

Coach continued, "Okay, other than Jonathan's error, that was a good scrimmage. Way to hustle on the field! I don't need to remind you that we're facing Sacred Heart in two weeks and again at homecoming, and I want to wipe the field with those bleeding hearts. Got it?"

We played for pure love of the game. We played for pride in East Bay Christian Academy. We played for Protestants everywhere. We all got it.

"Thanks for trying out today. I'll post the varsity and JV lineups tomorrow at practice. Go grab the balls and cones and then hit the showers!" Coach dismissed us. I was just about to head off the field with Pete when he called me back.

"You lost your balance? C'mon, Cooper. I've seen you

make that shot a million times." Coach took his sunglasses off and stared at me.

The heat on the field rose about fifteen degrees. "It's my ankle. I sprained it a few weeks ago at camp. It's better but not quite healed."

"So what are we talking about? Can you play or not?" Coach Thomas was a bottom-line kind of guy. He taught mathematical statistics as a way of supporting his soccer addiction. *Bench him? Cut him? Rotate him?* I could see him running the numbers, calculating the highest percentage for success.

"I can play," I said. And then to make sure he believed it, I added. "Really, Coach. I can play."

"Okay, Cooper, but you need to tell me if you can't keep up."

Pete smiled, his ice blue eyes and white blond hair a stark contrast to his tanned skin. He'd spent his summer outside, no doubt honing his soccer moves. "Don't worry, Coach, Jonathan'll be in fighting shape in no time." Pete slapped me on the back.

Luke, the transfer from Minnetonka Public, walked up and handed Coach a stack of cones. "Yeah, I heard Jonathan spent most of the summer practicing his *ball-handling skills*."

The trembling started in my cleats and worked its way through my aching ankle, my tensed calf and thigh muscles, my pounding chest until it finally shook loose the fear that had slowly eaten away the resolve I'd found at Spirit Lake Bible camp.

What would I do if anyone at school found out the truth about me?

CHAPTER THREE

Grass smashed into my face. The scent of dirt flooded my nose. Their voices stabbed me, sharp and quick, worse than the pain in my ankle. I lifted a hand to shield my eyes from the glaring sun and saw that I was lying on the ground, surrounded by shadowy bodies that inched closer, step by step.

"Tell me what else you heard about Jonathan." A Pete-shaped shadow turned to look at a Luke-shaped shadow.

"I heard he was—"

Their heads bent together. Faces twisted in disgust.

My whole body started shaking.

No, I was being shaken.

"Jonathan, honey, it's time to get up."

I blinked into the early morning light and stared at my mother in her bathrobe, smiling down at me.

"Don't want to be late for your first day of school, do you?" She flicked her fingers through my hair, tender, like I was still a kid.

I rolled over, turning my head into my pillow, and groaned. I'd tell her the truth, except she wasn't dealing too well with truth lately.

"It will be good for you to see your friends and get your life back to normal."

"Uh-huh." I knew what she wanted. For last summer to be erased.

Just a month ago I had told Ian, my newly acquired boyfriend, that I was done hiding who I was, and I'd meant it at the time. Now, still trying to shake the dream, all I wanted was for the truth to never come out.

Mom, I wanted to tell her, *normal is just another illusion.*

The door closed softly behind her. I threw off the covers and sat at the edge of my bed and found myself face-to-face with reality, the varsity soccer team roster on my nightstand. I picked up the piece of paper. The East Bay Crusaders in all their glory. I scanned the familiar names of my friends until I stuck on the one name that had me worried. Luke Williams, the new kid.

I heard his voice again. *Jonathan spent most of the summer practicing his ball-handling skills.* My hand tightened on the sheet of paper as I struggled to control the panic that had been building over the past two weeks of soccer practice where I had worked on scissor kicks and Luke had perfected dropping hints. He had it down cold.

"Dear Lord, please protect me from—" Cold sweat broke out over my body. Was it okay to pray for God to protect me from the fallout of something the Bible called an abomination? "Please God," I began again, but my head spun and my chest tightened. I took a deep breath and found the words. "I'm afraid. Please be with me today."

I put down the soccer roster, reached for my Bible, and opened to 1 Peter 5:7 where I entrusted his picture to the verse. *Cast all your worries on him, for he cares about you.* Covered in Kevlar, Dad leaned against a tank. Sand, like danger, swirled around him, but still he smiled.

"I think Luke knows," I told my father, but he wasn't there. He was just a voice in my mind, telling me the same thing he told me every time I freaked out about something. Most of the time it even worked.

You have to be strong and face your fears, Jon. Courage is endurance for one moment more!

In Dad's world, there was one sure test of a man's strength. I dropped to the ground, my weight balancing on my toes and splayed hands.

One…two…three…

Up and down, up and down, my arms pumped until beads of sweat converged on my forehead and dripped on the floor.

44…45…46…

Up and down, up and down, my arms pumped until my pulse thundered in my ears and my breath blew from my dry mouth in hard blasts, parting the hair that fell across my face.

76…77…78…

Up and down, up and down, I ignored my screaming shoulders and tried to summon Dad's strength while Mom shouted, "Jon, are you getting ready?"

121…122…123…

Up and down, up and down, I continued even when my arms started to tremble as Mom opened the door. "School starts in less than thirty minutes! What are you doing?"

165…166…167…

Up and down, up and down, I endured though pain shot down my neck and my arm muscles seized.

168…

"Jonathan?" Mom stood with her hands planted on her hips, frowning at me.

169…

"Fine, if you're late, you're just going to have to face the consequences." The door shut behind her.

170.

I collapsed, unable to stay with the pain for one moment more. My father's record was 500 push-ups. I'd counted them myself. One hundred and seventy was a personal best, but all I could think about, as I sucked air on the floor, were the 330 that separated us.

❖

The wealthy family of a fallen marine founded East Bay Christian Academy seventy years ago. Lieutenant Lance Porter died in the Battle of Tarawa in 1943, and his parents, devastated by the loss of their son, razed their sprawling estate along the east bay of Lake Minnetonka and built a school dedicated to two things: God and Country. Red brick after red brick, they built a fortress and filled it with stained glass windows and dark mahogany woodwork. The first thing to greet anyone who stepped into the main entrance of the school was a huge wall mural that depicted a battlefield. *For thou hast girded me with strength unto the battle: thou hast subdued under me those that rose up against me.* The quotation from Psalms 18:39 promised victory to some; defeat to others. It was all a matter of perspective.

Annual tuition at East Bay Christian Academy topped nearly every private college in Minnesota and every state university. Marine brats like me went on scholarships that reduced the tuition by eighty percent, making it almost affordable if my family swapped meatloaf for steaks. It was a small sacrifice according to Mom.

I parked Dad's car and glanced at the rearview mirror. My blue-and-white-striped tie was crooked so I straightened it. My hair was too long, too shaggy for East Bay standards, but I was probably okay. I turned off the car and looked at my watch. 8:05 a.m. Crap! I sprinted across the parking lot and up the steps of the school. Through the atrium and down the main hallway, past the school office to the stairwell that led to the lower level where my first class, art exploration, had begun ten minutes ago.

"Mr. Cooper, I did not receive a call from your mother informing me that you would be late for school."

I turned to face the consequences. "Hi, Principal Hardin. Yeah, I know."

"What do you have to say for yourself?" He pulled himself up to his full height, which was approximately 5'4", though it was a well-known East Bay Christian Academy urban legend that Principal Hardin wore lifts in his shoes and was actually shorter than Prince. Or the Artist formerly known as Prince. Or whatever, the dude who owned the purple house in Chanhassen. I liked his music, but I'd never admit that to any of the guys on my soccer team. Just one more thing I hoped they'd never find out about me.

"I'm sorry. It won't happen again."

Principal Hardin crossed his arms and rocked back on his high heels. "I believe an hour detention should ensure that you are motivated to carry out that promise. After school today. Mr. Gilchrist is supervising. Report to his room directly after your last class, and, Mr. Cooper, I would not recommend showing up late."

"But I've got soccer practice after school. We're playing our first game against Sacred Heart on Thursday."

He wavered. "I see. I suppose I could let you off with a warning this time." His eyes shone, and I knew I had him. "Make me proud on Thursday, Jonathan!" he shouted after me as I headed down the stairs to the lower level that held the art classroom, the boiler room, and, according to rumors, the ghosts of at least three dead kids. It was creepy in a dank and dark sort of way, but it was also a place where students were free to smoke, swear, flirt, fart, fling paint, or be late, and no one, least of all Ms. Owens, the art teacher, cared. I loved it.

"Good morning, Jonathan! How was your summer?" Ms. Owens chirped as she wove through the bodies and canvases.

"Hi, Ms. Owens. It was—"

I still wasn't sure how to describe the past summer so I held my camera out to her as my response. She flipped through the black-and-white shots I'd taken at Spirit Lake Bible Camp, where I had been trying to *see* the light.

"Beautiful, Jonathan!" Ms. Owens beamed at me. "Your interpretation of shadow is impressive. There are a few photographers whose work I'd like you to study this semester. Has anyone seen my pen?" Ms. Owens patted her pockets while the class tried and failed to stifle their giggles. It was an estimate, I grant you, but there appeared to be three pencils and two paintbrushes sticking out of the bird's nest of hair that resided on top of Ms. Owens's head.

"You can borrow mine." A girl whose liberal interpretation of our school uniform included black fishnet nylons and heavy combat boots stepped away from her canvas and handed a pen to Ms. Owens.

Wonderful. Another year of art with Sketch Mallory, aka *the weirdest girl in the whole school.*

"Thank you. You're such a dear." Ms. Owens jotted down the names for me.

I took the slip of paper and headed to the newly remodeled computer station shared by photographers and graphic artists in the far corner of the art room known to everyone as the "red light district." Digital photography may have made the darkroom outdated, but its nickname had survived and even taken on new layers of meaning.

Ms. Owens walked over to Sketch to return the pen. "Oh

my, what are you painting?" She did a double take at the canvas that looked like a snapshot of a crime scene.

"What it feels like to be under fire."

I put my camera bag down on the corner of the computer station next to a guy I didn't know whose books, notebooks, and backpack were taking up the entire table. I shot a dirty look at him and walked over to check out Sketch's painting.

Streaks of clotted red bled like an open wound down the canvas. Harsh lines of black skidded across it, their trajectory broken by the red that seeped down, and I wondered how she could have known the paint would drip in exactly that pattern. I took a closer look at the weird girl. Dark eyes. Black jagged hair she'd probably attacked with an X-Acto knife jutted in odd angles around her face. She took a deep breath, shook her shoulders, and moved in closer to the canvas. She flicked a subtle shade of rose along what looked to be a hollow bone that dripped angry ribbons of pain. That's when I saw it, the dove struggling to fly. One wing broken and bleeding.

"Whoa." I sucked in the turpentine-flavored air. "What do you call it?"

She stepped away from the canvas, her face a kaleidoscopic splatter of it all, and looked at me. "*The* Jonathan Cooper is talking to me? You're kidding, right?"

What was she talking about? *The* Jonathan Cooper? "Huh? What?" Damn, that shade of rose changed everything. "It's an amazing painting."

"Hmm." She eyed me the way the spider looks at a bug caught in its web. "Okay, what the hell. I'll play. I call it *Dying Dove.*"

"How do you know it's going to die? I mean, it might survive." I studied the awful, beautiful painting.

"Of course the dove dies. The dove always dies." A male voice spoke behind me. I hadn't seen the guy from the computer station walk over. Hadn't felt him standing there, looking at the painting over my shoulder.

I turned to look at him. Tall, thin, sandy blond hair. Dark eyes framed in tortoiseshell glasses. Who was this guy? "Says who?"

"Says me." He straightened his bow tie.

"And you are?"

"Mason Kellerman."

"You new?"

He stared at me, his face hardening. "Uh...we had two classes together last year."

"Oh, sorry." I turned back to the painting. "I still think the dove lives."

"Yeah, well, you're clueless. The dove is toast." Sketch sneered. "Why don't you go fiddle with your viewfinder some more, Mr. Jonathan Cooper? Take a few snapshots of the cheerleaders doing somersaults. Here's a hint. Use high speed film and you might even catch a crotch shot." She dismissed me and turned back to her *Dying Dove* or whatever the hell she decided was a good enough name to capture the feeling of being under fire. I wandered back to my corner of the computer station and looked at my watch.

It was 8:45 a.m. I'd already been late to school, almost gotten detention, and now it looked like my favorite class was going to be ruined by those two a-holes. The day had to get better, right?

CHAPTER FOUR

My second class was American literature with Mr. Gilchrist. Rumor had it this was his fiftieth year at East Bay. Whether that was true or not, the antique English teacher certainly was as much a part of the foundation of the place as the brick and mortar.

He nodded at me as I walked into the classroom and sat next to Pete and Ethan. Mason sauntered in and took a seat in the front row. I was about to fill the guys in about the dorky kid with the bow tie in my art class when Mr. Gilchrist stepped away from the whiteboard and cleared his throat. That was his signal for *shut the hell up and pay attention.*

"Ladies and gentlemen, welcome to eleventh grade American literature. I've written one of my favorite literary quotes on the board to begin the year. Let's take a look at it, shall we?" Mr. Gilchrist read aloud. "*No man, for any considerable period, can wear one face to himself, and another to the multitude, without finally getting bewildered as to which may be the true.* Now, ladies and gentlemen, can anyone identify this quote? Better yet if you could tell me what it means."

Mason's hand shot up from the front row.

"Yes, Mr. Kellerman?"

"It's a quote from *The Scarlet Letter* by Nathaniel Hawthorne. It means that trying to be someone you're not doesn't work. In the end you wind up not knowing who you are at all."

I stared at Mason. Maybe there was more to him than bow ties after all.

"Mr. Kellerman is right. We will be reading *The Scarlet Letter* by Nathaniel Hawthorne this semester. It is the story of Hester Prynne, a young married woman who travels alone to Salem, Massachusetts, during the height of the Puritan settlement and has an affair with the local minister, Reverend Dimmesdale. She conceives a child and, refusing to identify the baby's father, is sentenced to wearing a bright red letter A on her chest."

"Jeez, spoiler alert!" Pete leaned toward me, his hand cupped around his mouth. He needed a lesson on whispering because Gilchrist shot a dirty look at us.

"Mr. Mitchell, if you could stem your commentary, I will gladly tell you why I am summarizing the plot of the book before you even read it. *The Scarlet Letter* is a complex story, published in 1850. You will find its language challenging, its pace frustrating." Mr. Gilchrist's face deepened into shades of rose, then burgundy the longer he ranted. "So be it. I do not expect you to like it. I do, however, expect you to learn from it. What determines guilt? What justifies breaking the law of man? Of God? It is important that you understand what is at stake as you approach *The Scarlet Letter*. You may thank me for the plot summary on Friday when you take the quiz on the first three chapters."

The class groaned. A girl in the front row raised her hand.

"Yes?" Mr. Gilchrist took a deep breath, the flush on his

face retreating. How he could get so worked up over a musty old book mystified me.

"I don't get it," she said. "Why the letter A? Why is that such a big deal?"

Guess who raised his hand again?

"Yes, Mr. Kellerman?"

"The A stands for adultery. The sentence is having her sin on display for everyone to see. As long as she wears the letter A, the only person Hester Prynne will ever be is an adulteress."

"Mr. Kellerman is correct again. And now, please open your books and begin reading."

"They made this into a movie, you know," Pete whispered to me. "I'm talking full-on Demi Moore nipple action. Why don't we blow this off and just watch the movie?"

"Not a chance in the world." My cell phone vibrated in my pocket. I pulled it out and tucked it under my desk just in case. "Gilchrist would bust us for sure."

I opened the text.

Ian!

Hey, I thought of you today. You do crazy things to me.

I opened the attached picture and shoved my cell back in my jeans. Which was where Ian should have kept the subject matter of the photo. Damn camera phones.

"Bro, what's up? You just turned about ten shades of red," Pete whispered to me.

"Mom wants me to grab more blue tape on my way home."

"She's painting again? That's like, what? The third room in two weeks?"

Mr. Gilchrist cleared his throat and stared at Pete and me. I spent the rest of the hour, excruciatingly slow second after second, reading and thinking about the Hawthorne quote.

No man, for any considerable period, can wear one face to himself, and another to the multitude. I snuck side glances at Pete and Ethan. Did a soccer team count as a multitude?

The rest of the day was normal enough. Mathematical statistics with Coach Thomas. Boring! History. So-So. Lunch. It was a nice surprise when, for once, Pete, Ethan, Brandon, Zack, Austin (plus their varied assortment of girlfriends) and I were all in lunch period B. We sat at our usual table, the long one by the window where we could at least look outside at the east bay of Lake Minnetonka even if we couldn't be there. No matter what crap came out of the lunchroom, we got a regular serving of freedom by looking out that window. Best of all, Luke was not in lunch period B.

But he was in the hallway outside the cafeteria after lunch, one foot kicked behind him and perched on a locker as he waved his hands and told a story. They followed him, the group of guys that surrounded him. They followed his hands, his words, his eyes as he watched me walk past the office, the trophy case, the girls' bathroom, the water fountain until I ducked into Frau Schmidt's classroom and heard someone whisper my name. But by seventh hour science with Ms. Jennings I'd convinced myself I was letting paranoia get the best of me.

Ms. Jennings looked like a timid little field mouse with her thick glasses and pale complexion, but she was actually fierce—a reputation that was not based on rumor. It was a fact that she had taken on the board of trustees two years ago and won the right to teach evolution. She didn't believe intelligent design was good science. She also didn't believe in seating charts, so Pete, Ethan, Luke, and I claimed the back row.

"All right, class, we're going to study a controversial subject this semester, but one that I believe is important for you to know." Ms. Jennings began her lecture. "Specifically, Darwin's theory of evolution. Charles Darwin was a scientist who lived in England during the 1800s. He is best known for his belief that all creatures come from common ancestors, but that various species acclimated to different environments that posed unique challenges. This caused them to evolve in diverse ways until they barely resembled one another." Ms. Jennings paced as she lectured, but I didn't mind.

"You mean like monkeys and humans, right?" a girl in the front row asked.

"That's right, Ashley. Darwin believed that all primates— monkeys, apes, gorillas, and *homo sapiens*—have the same ancestor, but evolved into uniquely different types of animals because of their environments and circumstances." Ms. Jennings lectured and paced, lectured and paced.

And that's when it happened. Beside me, Luke whispered, "I hear you know a lot about *homo* sapiens, Cooper. In fact, I hear you're an expert on the subject!"

I shot a glance at him. He leaned toward me, the corners of his lips twisted into some bold-faced lie of a smile. His eyes narrowed and told the truth. I swiveled in my seat and stared at Ms. Jennings.

"Darwin's theories are based on one fundamental fact: The world is in a state of constant change. We see evidence of this in our evolution as a species and as a society. Scientists have come to believe that this change is inevitable and pointless to resist. We need only look to extinct species to realize that those who do not change do not survive. Darwin called this process natural selection." Ms. Jennings uncapped a marker and turned to the whiteboard. The room filled with an acrid scent and the sound of squeaking as she outlined Darwin's *The Origin of Species*.

CHAPTER FIVE

I turned my puce-colored Honda (make that Dad's puce-colored Honda on loan to me while he was in Afghanistan) onto Cherry Lane and parked in the narrow driveway in front of Number 63, the white story-and-a-half bungalow with black shutters and a cranberry door, where I've lived my whole life. The first floor belonged to my parents, Linda and Butch Cooper, Sunday school teacher and badass marine, respectively. The half-story upstairs was all mine. Most marine brats move around a lot growing up, but not me. Mom agreed to marry Dad twenty years ago on two conditions: a) he would not haul their family all around the United States, and b) any children they had would be raised Southern Baptist. Dad had fought in Desert Storm, Iraq, and Afghanistan. He'd conducted black ops into the heart of jihad territory and come out unscathed. Ask him and he'd tell you that the only battle wounds he'd ever gotten had been the result of domestic fire.

"Thank goodness you're home!" I found Mom perched on a ladder in the kitchen. Or what was left of the kitchen. Tarps covered everything. The table, the counters, the floors. Blue tape ran the length of the floorboards and framed the cupboards.

"You're painting another room?" I stared at her.

"Correction. *We're* painting another room. Grab a brush."

I dipped a brush into the can of "Yellow Tulips," and slathered paint into the corners...around the door frame... behind the refrigerator...and around the cupboards.

Ping!

I dug my cell out of my pocket. Another text from Ian.

Thinking about you. Hard as a—

"Jonathan, you missed a spot! Look, right there!" Mom pointed at a patch of gray that poked through the hideous yellow. "Stop rushing and focus. You don't want to have to repaint this all by yourself, do you?"

"No, ma'am." I tucked the cell back in my pocket. One swipe and the offending bit of gray disappeared.

Mom wrestled the ladder over to the last wall and eyed me. "What's wrong with you?"

"Just nerves, I guess. Big game on Thursday. I wish Dad could be there. I can always hear him shouting from the bleachers."

"I miss him too, Jonathan. I'm sure he'll call us soon." Her face softened and she crossed the small kitchen to wrap her arms around me.

"Are you going to tell him? About me and—" There are things to say when your mother is hugging you for the first time in a month. This was not one of them. Mom stiffened in my arms and pulled away.

"Why don't you go do your homework? I can finish this." She dipped her brush in the tray.

The scent of paint chased Butler, our fifteen-year-old tuxedo cat, and me up the stairs to my bedroom where I shut the door on my mother and her crusade to cover up reality with a fresh coat of paint.

"You rubbed up against a wall again, didn't you?" I

laughed, noticing the streaks of yellow that covered Butler's left side. They joined the bits of maroon from the living room and the sage green from the hallway.

I threw my backpack in the corner and crashed on my unmade bed, the camouflage bedspread half on the bed and half on the floor. Don't get me wrong. I missed Dad, but there were some advantages to his deployment. Taking a pass on the morning bed inspection was one of them. I stared at the poster of David Beckham in his Manchester United uniform that hung on the slanted wall over my bed (the pictures of him in his underwear were safely hidden between the mattresses) and opened the text.

Ian: *Thinking about you. Hard as a rock.*

For once, the attached picture didn't make me rush to hit delete. It was an actual rock.

Ha, ha! How RU? I replied.

A few seconds passed before I heard the familiar *ping.*

Ian: *I continue to suffer under the rule of Matilda the Hun and Fidel Castro.*

I didn't know how to reply to that. The fact that Ian's parents had kicked him out when they found him looking at gay porn pretty much defined shitty parenting. The Department of Child Welfare's solution to temporarily place Ian with Tilly and Frank Castell, redneck dairy farmers in rural Wisconsin, while his parents received counseling was, in my opinion, no solution at all. Every night, I prayed that Ian's parents would have a change of heart and that he would be able to go back home. Even if he would never admit it, I knew it was what he wanted most of all. So far, that prayer had gone unanswered.

In the time it took me not to respond, he sent another picture. This time it was not of a rock. When would Ian ever figure out that close-ups of dicks were not sexy? Now David Beckham's bulging pecs…

You are a dick! I texted him.

He responded, *Yeah, but you love me.*

And he was right. I did love him. Meeting Ian at Spirit Lake Bible Camp last summer had been like waking up one morning and looking in the mirror and actually recognizing the person looking back at me. I found myself the day I found Ian. Unfortunately, since camp ended, he might as well have been living on the moon. Both of us were afraid of being overheard talking on the phone, so texting (and the occasional sexting) was the thin thread that kept us connected. What can I say? The situation wasn't exactly ideal.

I gripped my cell. My thumbs hovered over the screen.

I miss your face.

Ping! He replied right away. Finally! A picture I wanted to see. Red curls. An uncountable number of freckles. Eyes the color of emeralds. I felt the blood drain from my brain.

"Jonathan, it's finished. Come take a look!" Mom shouted from downstairs.

GTG, I texted. *Give my love to Matilda and Fidel. Lol! Love you!*

Mom stood in the middle of the kitchen, her hands on both hips. "I love it! It makes me think of springtime! What do you think?"

Blech.

"It's great! Really, um, tulipy," I lied.

"Oh, by the way, I picked up a book for you from the library." Mom dug under the tarp that covered the kitchen table and came out with a book titled *Claiming Your True Identity in Christ.* "It was written by men who have faced what you're, well, fighting…and God helped them to change."

"Thanks." I scanned the inside jacket. "I think."

❖

"Dig deep, guys. We got these pansies!" Coach Thomas shouted Thursday afternoon from the sidelines. The score was tied three to three with Pete leading our forwards on an assault deep in Sacred Heart turf. I hung back, covering the penalty box. I shot a glance around the field at the crowd of blue and white jerseys on my right. A tidal wave of East Bay fans. I looked to my left at the firewall of red and gold. Sacred Heart fans.

Then I spotted him, number thirteen. The boy in the red and gold jersey. At the midfield line and moving fast. I mean, *damn,* he was fast. He darted past Ethan. I ran a few steps forward. He twirled around Luke like he wasn't even there.

"Coop, you got this?" Pete shouted at me from behind the midfield line. I nodded and ran for the guy. He spotted me and planted his left foot. I lunged forward into the path of the ball, except it never appeared. I swiveled to look in disbelief as he shot the ball to the left behind his body with his right foot and darted around me toward the goal. I twisted to follow. Pain shot up my calf. I slowed. Just for a second. Turns out that was all I had.

The ref blew his whistle.

Game over. Four-three, Sacred Heart.

Coach looked at me, his face a deep shade of purple, and walked off the field. I limped into the locker room, glad the ordeal was over only to discover it had just begun.

"What the hell happened? Did he trip over his dick or something?" I heard the frustration in Pete's voice behind the row of lockers.

I didn't need to see him to picture his face. Red from exertion and fury. I didn't blame him.

"Way I heard it, he tripped over another dude's dick." Luke's words floated over the wall of lockers on the steam from the shower room to where I stood, glued to the floor by the door, gripping the handle and praying to die.

❖

Mom said all the things moms are supposed to say. *It's just a game. You did your best and that's all that matters. I'm proud of you for trying.* She stopped when my bedroom door slammed shut in her face. I looked around for something to kick or throw. I picked up my backpack and contemplated chucking it through my window when I remembered we had a quiz on the first three chapters of *The Scarlet Letter* in the morning. The proverbial icing on the crap cupcake, right?

An hour later, I lay in my bed, Butler curled between my feet and purring so loud I could barely concentrate on chapter three of *The Scarlet Letter*. I'd just reached the point where Hester Prynne recognized her husband, returned from the dead, to witness her public shaming.

"Very soon, however, his look became keen and penetrative. A writhing horror twisted itself across his features, like a snake gliding swiftly over them…"

I flung my copy of *The Scarlet Letter* across my room. It bounced off the poster of David Beckham, pecs and all, and almost took out Butler, who hissed in protest. Hester Prynne's whack job of a husband, Luke, Pete, and my entire soccer team could suck it. They were the reason I was forced to wear one face to myself and another at school.

The sound of Mom's fist knocking on my door made me jump. "Jonathan? Are you all right?" I could hear her concern, but it didn't change anything.

"Yeah, I'm fine. Why wouldn't I be?" The lies, I noticed, were getting easier to tell.

I dropped to the ground and assumed the push-up position.

One…two…three…

Up and down, up and down, I pushed.

71…72…73…

Up and down, up and down, I kept going even when my arms trembled and pain shot down my spine.

156…157…158…

Up and down, up and down, I pushed until my shoulders burned and my heart threatened to pound out of my chest.

250…

I dropped to the ground, spent, but halfway to the goal.

CHAPTER SIX

I am swimming toward the surface. Pushing against the weight that pulls me under. Shadows move above me, blocking the muted white light. A voice pings through the layers.

"There you are, Jonathan! Welcome back." It is a woman's voice. Creaking and lilting like an old person's rocking chair.

The light flickers, and I am suddenly looking at the world through a red lens.

"I need to question this patient." That voice I know. The blotch of blue that won't go away no matter how hard I scrub.

The red haze retreats into a soft white light.

"You may talk to him when I say so, Detective," the creaky-voiced woman says. I crack my eyelids to see if she is as old as she sounds. Wrinkled and short, gray-haired and liver-spotted she is, but that does not make her weak. She stands, fists planted on her hips, and glares up at the blotch in blue. She glares him out of the room. I sigh, but it sputters into a cough.

"Here, take a sip." She holds the straw to my lips and I drink because a) it's heaven, and b) as long as I am drinking, no one can expect me to talk.

"My name is Grace. I'm here to help you," she says while I swallow.

She pulls up a chair and sits beside my bed. Every few minutes, she reaches across and holds the glass for me. I drink until I can't drink anymore. A shiver crawls across my skin.

"Are you cold?" she asks, and I nod. She stands and crosses the room to open the closet where my clothes hang. Jeans and a Manchester United jersey. They were clean once. Now they are covered in blood smears. Grace finds the extra blanket on the top shelf where a glittering crown, now bent, sits. She looks at me, one scraggly caterpillar eyebrow raised in a question I can't answer. She shrugs, puts the crown back on the shelf, and closes the closet door.

"Better?" she asks, laying the extra blanket across me.

"Yeah, thank you," I say, feeling positively chatty.

"You're welcome. I really am here for you, Jonathan, and believe me, you need help. There's a detective standing right outside your room."

"I know, but I can't tell him anything." I roll on my side and stare at the silver bars that trap me in this bed. Slowly, back and forth, my body rocks. I'd stop, but, small comfort though it is, I can't give it up.

"He has some questions for you about what happened. I can keep him away for a while, but I'm afraid you're going to have to talk to him soon."

"Don't you understand? I *can't* tell him anything!" My rocking quickens. I don't even try to hide it.

"I see." Minutes pass. Her pen scratches across the paper. I wonder what she's writing so I peek. She catches me and smiles.

"What's the last thing you remember?" Her glasses slip down her nose. She scowls and pushes them up.

I close my eyes and try to wade through the blur to find the one solid image I can hold on to.

"Ian," I say. "The last thing I remember is dancing with Ian." And then the light glints off the silver bars that line my bed and I slip away again.

CHAPTER SEVEN

It didn't surprise me when I got a text from Coach Thomas asking to talk to me before school. I found him in his classroom behind his desk, red pen in hand and peering back and forth from the key to the quiz he'd given us in statistical mathematics and a pile of papers. Damn. The answer to number four was false. Why do I always second-guess my first instinct?

"I'm the reason we lost to Sacred Heart," I said it before he could.

"True," he mumbled, not looking up from the pile of papers on his desk.

I shifted my weight, wondering if his answer was meant for me or the poor schlep who'd just missed question number seven. "You should probably bench me."

Coach lifted his head. "Also true, but I'm not going to. I'm seventy-five percent sure that you are a greater asset to this team than you are a liability, so I'm swapping you and Ethan. He can cover the midfield. I'm putting you on defense where you won't have to run quite so much." He picked up the next test, swore when he read the first answer, and picked up his pen. I took that as my dismissal.

Which made it official. I was on the defense, a fact that became more obvious as the bell rang, signaling the five-minute warning to the start of first hour.

Paranoia is when you think everyone is talking about you and they're not. Hell is when you think everyone is talking about you and they are.

I realized this as I walked down the staircase to the lower level of the school and instantly felt the hellishness of it all when Pete and Brandon walked out of the boiler room, a cloud of cigarette smoke dissipating behind them.

"Hey, guys, Hardin's on the prowl again. I think he's heading down here." I thought I was warning *my friends* until I saw Pete's face. Cold and blank, his eyes locked with mine for a few seconds too long to leave much doubt.

"You should be watching your own back, Cooper," he said as he walked up the stairs.

There are, I discovered, many layers to hell.

I learned this fact when I walked into the art room and all conversation stopped. Heat hijacked my face as I made my way to the red light district where Mason's crap littered the computer station. Ribbon, buttons, feathers, and a *Vogue* magazine had taken over the counter. *What the hell are you designing?* I almost asked, but he turned away from me. I cleared a space for my camera and sat next to him on the bench.

I inserted the memory card and was flipping through the black-and-white shots of Spirit Lake Bible Camp when I heard a cough behind me.

"What?" I turned around and found Sketch standing, a feathering brush in one hand.

"Is it true?" she asked, pointing the brush at me.

"Is what true?"

"I told you he wouldn't have the balls to man up," Mason said to Sketch.

"Quit being a douche, Mason. He's one of us." She flicked her brush at him, splattering him with purple paint.

"This is a new shirt, Sketch! I know you don't have any respect for fashion, but some of us do! And he most certainly is NOT one of us."

"It's a school uniform shirt, for God's sakes, Mason. They're like $10.99, and he's one of us if I say he's one of us. You know Hardin said he'd consider our request if we had three members. Jonathan's our third." Sketch took a rag and tried to wipe the paint off Mason's shirt.

"Dab! Don't wipe! Stop. Just stop! You're making it worse." Mason grabbed the rag from her hand. "And don't tell me you bought that line. For God's sake, Sketch, the guy is the principal of eBay High. He would have sold you any line to get you out of his office."

"Um, third what?" I asked.

"Shut up!" they said in unison.

It was bizarre watching the two of them argue, especially since I had no clue what they were arguing about. Mason with his purple paint-smeared shirt, his eyes widening behind his glasses as he spotted Sketch—her combat boot raised and aimed at his shin—moments before an impact that set him yelping.

The argument never was settled, thanks to the fact that Ms. Owens investigated episodes of yelping in her classroom.

Things did not improve as the day went on.

"Today, we are going to talk about our protagonist, Hester Prynne. A protagonist is often referred to as the hero of the story. What qualities does Hester Prynne possess that qualify her to be our story's hero?" Old Man Gilchrist asked at the beginning of second hour.

"Bravery," the girl who had asked about the letter A suggested. "I don't think I could do it. Day after day with everyone staring at me like that."

"Strength." Ethan glanced at me from across the room

where he sat next to Pete. Unsurprisingly, all the seats near them had been taken by the time I'd walked into American lit. "Hester Prynne stands up against all of them. Chick's got balls."

"Courage," I said. Old Man Gilchrist nodded.

"Bravery and courage are the same thing, asshat," Pete said. I chose to believe the laughter from the class was mainly due to the fact that he had said *asshat* in Old Man Gilchrist's classroom and gotten away with it.

"Actually, they're not." Mason spoke up from three seats away from me. He winked at me and twirled a pencil between his fingers. "Bravery is doing something scary without thinking about it. Like a firefighter running into a burning building. He's so hopped up on adrenaline he thinks he's Superman or something. But courage is knowing you can get squished like a bug at any moment and facing the scary thing anyway. It's Jimmy Olsen running into the burning building."

Old Man Gilchrist nodded, agreeing with Mason, which was awesome because I had just blurted out some asshat answer without thinking.

Mathematical statistics was a small relief when I discovered that I'd managed to pull off a B+ on the quiz. Fourth hour history was still about old dead people who did boring old stuff that didn't have a thing to do with my life. Still, I wouldn't have minded staying there all day, but of course, the bell rang, signaling the inevitable.

I made my way down the packed hallway, pinballing off the zigzagging bodies, to the cafeteria—the deepest layer of hell. A place crammed with people I was certain knew everything about me. I stumbled through the lunch line, held my plate out for whatever the lunch lady felt like plopping on it, and walked over to the table with the view of the lake.

"Sorry, Coop, that seat's taken," Brandon said just as I was about to sit down next to him.

"Taken? Okay." I moved to the right, leaving an open seat between us, and began to sit.

"That one's taken too." Zack sneered.

"In fact, all these seats are taken." Pete swung his arm to indicate every seat at our table. "Think of this as a fag-free zone."

"W-w-what?" I stood there, feet glued to the ground.

"Wait, what are you talking about?" Ethan shifted on the bench to look at Pete. "Jonathan always sits with us."

"You heard what Luke said about him." Pete's face twisted in disgust.

"What I heard was some kid we don't even know slamming one of my best friends!" Ethan stood up, his eyes locked on Pete. A hush fell over the cafeteria.

Pete leaned forward. "Are you sure that's all you two are, Ethan? *Friends?*"

Ethan sat on the bench with a thud. His mouth opened and closed, but no words came out. I turned to leave, but he reached for me, his hand clasping my arm. "Wait, Jonathan. You don't have to—"

"Yeah, Ethan. I'm pretty sure I do." Our eyes connected. "It's okay."

He released my arm, and I discovered there was nothing and no one holding me to the table with the view of the lake. I wandered away, scanning tables, until I reached the middle of the cafeteria and stood there, holding a tray with a plate full of gross.

"Yo, Jonathan," a familiar voice called my name, "are you going to stand there drooling over a bunch of butt cracks or are you going to sit down and eat?"

I walked over to the small table in the corner and sat next to Sketch and Mason.

"You okay?" She looked at my face. "You look like you're going to hurl."

"Fine."

"I'm just saying, if you're going to hurl, I'd appreciate some warning." Sketch slid a few inches to the left.

"I'm fine!" I turned to Mason and changed the subject. "Thanks for bailing me out in American lit. What are you, like a genius or something?"

Sketch stuck a finger in her mouth and made a gagging sound.

"Now he notices me in a class." Mason sprinkled Parmesan cheese on his lasagna, a slight smile playing at the corners of his mouth. "Is it because you're finally out?"

"W-what?" I stammered. "I don't know what you're talking about!"

"Well, I do," Sketch said. "Word has it Luke, the new transfer kid from Minnetonka Public, knows for a fact you had all sorts of raging gay sex with a guy at soccer camp last summer. Says he has proof."

I wanted to scream. I wanted to throw my tray across the cafeteria. I almost hurled.

"I heard it was two guys and it was full on anal wham-bam-thank-you-sir." Mason butchered more than a stupid rhyme. "I also heard you caught some STD."

I gripped my fork and counted to ten. "It was a *Bible* camp, and sure, I hung around with a guy named Ian, but we *did not* have raging gay sex, and I most certainly *do not have a STD!*"

"That's not what I heard." Mason lifted his box of chocolate milk to his lips.

"Well, I was there and I should know!" My voice rose

a few decibels. Heads turned. I mean, more heads turned. Actually, the few heads that weren't already staring at me, turned. "He was my friend. That's all!"

"Chill, gentlemen. The important thing right now is that Jonathan is about as popular as a case of herpes." Sketch pointed out the obvious. "Whether he has it or not is immaterial."

"It's not true!" I hissed.

Mason snorted. "Okay, Jonathan. Whatever you say." He took another sip.

I willed him to choke on his chocolate milk. Really I did. For one malicious moment, I saw it spewing out of his nostrils like a Hershey's geyser. It didn't happen, but it felt good to picture it.

Sketch erupted, "Knock it off, Mason. He's one of us now."

"*He's* one of us? Mr. *we were just friends, I swear?*"

Something thudded under the table, and Mason frowned at Sketch. "Quit kicking me!"

"Have you forgotten two years ago? When you went around telling everyone I was your girlfriend?" She threw a tomato slice at Mason. It hit him in the chest, leaving a red stain and a few seeds on his shirt when it dropped to the table.

"Wait, so you're not..." I looked at Mason.

"Going to sit here while this stain sets in." He stood and shot a lethal glance at Sketch.

"And you're...?" I asked Sketch after Mason headed toward the boys' bathroom.

"Does it matter?" She frowned. "Listen, Mason and I have been trying to form a Gay-Straight Alliance for two years, but school policy states a club must have a minimum of three charter members to form, and you know how much Hardin loves his school policies. What do you say...will you be our third?"

Somehow it didn't seem advisable to tell the only person willing to sit with me at lunch, especially since she was prone to throwing food, that I would rather contract a case of herpes.

❖

I spotted Luke after school, crouched down and digging something out of his locker, alone and off guard. I looked around for Pete or Zack or Brandon, anyone from the soccer team really. Nobody.

The temptation was overwhelming as I stood there behind him, my knee level with his shoulders, picturing it. His head smashing into the locker. Blood oozing down his goddamn face. So very tempting, and so not me. I knelt beside him.

"Consider this your official warning. Stop. Right now."

He swiveled to look at me. "What are you talking about?"

"The rumors you're spreading about me."

"It's only a rumor if it can't be proven." Luke smiled, keen and penetrative.

I dropped my voice, soft enough so only he could hear me. "See, that's just the thing, Luke. You weren't at Spirit Lake Bible Camp. In fact, *nobody* from school was there."

"Did I forget to mention?" He stood, closed the door of his locker, and turned to face me. "I saw my cousin at my family reunion in August. She was real interested to hear I was transferring to East Bay Christian Academy. Said she met someone at camp who goes here. A gay guy who made her look like a fool in some play. Maybe you remember her? MacKenzie?"

"MacKenzie?" I shrank back from the name. A girl, nobody special really. A pain in the ass with an inflated ego if truth be told, but MacKenzie had been at camp with Ian and me. She knew about us.

"Small world, isn't it, Cooper?" Luke took a few steps, then turned around and stared at me. "Oh, one last thing. You do know you weren't the only one with a camera at camp, right?"

He walked down the hallway while I stood there, a chill creeping over my body.

CHAPTER EIGHT

I woke up early Monday morning, which was completely unfair. Mondays were hard enough when they arrived on time. My phone seemed possessed as it gyrated and buzzed as text after text arrived. The first text I read was from Sketch.

Jonathan, DO NOT open any other text messages. Also, meet Mason and me in the art room. Be early.

I should have listened to her, but like an idiot, I opened the text from Pete. What had I expected? An apology? A miracle? Yeah, maybe a bit of both.

Dude, you won't believe what some creep is spreading about you at school.

It took a moment to appreciate the full genius of Pete's message. If I showed the text to anyone, he would just come off as a good guy, trying to warn his friend. While I would look like an ungrateful bastard.

I opened the attachment. Ugh, make that a skinny-dipping ungrateful bastard. I stared at the picture of two guys, bobbing in the lake, with the moonlight clearly showing their touching faces. Not a great night shot of a lake. It would have been better if the aperture had been widened, but it was good enough. I took a moment to wish all sorts of disease and pestilence on Luke and MacKenzie, and then I opened the other texts.

STBY, Bro from Brandon. For his tenth birthday, he'd been allowed to bring one friend to Wisconsin Dells for a weekend, and he had chosen me so, yeah, his *sucks to be you* text hurt.

Are you okay? Of course Ethan had texted me.

No, I am not okay! I wanted to respond, but he didn't need to get pulled into this mess.

I'm fine, Ethan, I texted. *Just a picture of me swimming. It doesn't mean anything.*

Just so you know, it wouldn't matter to me if it did, he responded.

I smiled, but didn't reply. There was only one person I could talk to about this, and it definitely wasn't Ethan.

I broke our no calling rule and dialed the number with the Wisconsin area code. Hearing his voice wouldn't delete the photo that for damn sure had made its way through the entire school body by now. It wouldn't transport him directly to my bedroom where he could wrap his arms around me and hold me together. But it would make me feel a little better. A little stronger. It always did.

"What are you doing?" he answered on the third ring, his voice tight and saying the words he wasn't. *What the hell are you doing calling me?*

"I'm sorry!" My words rushed out. "I just—I just needed to talk to you."

"Okay, hold on," he whispered, and then I heard the muffled sound of clanking pans and raised voices. I imagined him sitting in the kitchen of the farmhouse with Matilda the Hun and Fidel Castro, the sharp scent of barn hanging in the air. "It's a girl from school, that's who! Wants to know if I can pick her up. Can I take the truck this morning?" More muffled murmuring. Ian probably had his hand wrapped around his cell phone. "That's right, *a girl*. I can? Cool." When he spoke again, his voice came through loud and clear. "Hello? Yeah, I can pick you up. What happened to your car?"

It was my cue. But how could I tell him about Pete and the text and the picture? How could I fit all that into the few seconds Ian had created for us to talk?

"A guy at school knows about us. Don't ask me how, but he has a picture of us skinny-dipping. It's gone viral."

"You sure?" he asked.

"I've seen it." I heard his sharp intake of breath. Heard the soft *fuck* under his breath.

"There's only one thing you can do then. Wreck him. I mean, it—the car. You're going to have to haul its ass—sorry, Tilly—butt. Haul its butt to the wrecking yard and crush it until it's nothing but scrap metal. Seriously, you're gonna have to wreck him." He paused while I digested his advice. "Yeah, no problem. I'll be there soon to pick you up."

I heard the click. Listened to the dead air and wished he could be here soon. I wished it almost as much as I wished I could follow his advice.

Lord, please come to me! I prayed and waited for my racing pulse to slow. It didn't. My eyes fell on the latest book Mom had left on my nightstand. *Following His Footsteps*, written by a pastor who helped people leave the gay "lifestyle."

I stumbled out of bed and dropped to the ground.

One…two…three…

Up and down, up and down.

123…124…125…

Up and down, up and down. I pushed through the trembling of my arms. My back was straight. My breath was strong.

286…287…288…

Up and down, up and down, my hands cramped.

375…

Pain shot through my side, and I doubled over. Close, but not close enough.

Mom did a double take when I appeared in the kitchen a good half hour before usual. One look at my face and she forgot all about the cinnamon raisin bagel she was in the process of toasting.

"Jonathan! What's wrong?" she asked, as the cremated remains of her breakfast popped up. Smoke poured from the toaster.

"Nothing. Why?" I cracked the window, hoping the alarm would not go off.

"Don't *nothing* me. You've been crying." She stared at me, willing me to spill. As if.

"I have not. I just got something in my eye."

She grabbed the charred bagel and flung it into the sink. She sent a scathing glance at Butler, who didn't look the least bit concerned he was being unjustly blamed for wrecking breakfast as he batted a toy mouse around the floor.

"Sorry, I don't buy it. What's wrong?" Damn maternal instinct. Didn't she know if I *wanted* to talk about it, I *would* talk about it?

"I. Am. Fine!" I grabbed a granola bar and stormed out of the kitchen just as Butler pounced on the mouse and sank his teeth into it, unleashing the toy's high-pitched squeal. I hustled down the street and made it just in time to catch the bus to school, which would give me about forty minutes to meet with Sketch and Mason before first hour.

❖

"You are so royally screwed not even the Queen Mother could get you out of this." Mason leaned against the hot water registers, admiring a new pair of loafers. Like anyone at East Bay other than Mason wore loafers.

I was about to point that out to him when Sketch defended me.

"That's not helpful." She flung a dry eraser at him. "You agreed to help. If you're not with us, you are, by definition, against us. Though I must warn you that those who are against us may or may not live to regret that decision."

"Tell me you're not planning some kind of revenge." My stomach twisted at the thought of the three of us taking on Pete and his crew. The stuffed toy mouse had a better chance of eating Butler. "Seriously, I think we should just ride it out."

"No, I'm planning the ultimate kind of revenge. The type of revenge that involves itching powder and jockstraps, photos of them naked plastered all over the Internet, humiliation at its highest level." Her eyes shone with the fervor of one possessed.

For a fleeting moment, I saw it all in beautiful, Technicolor detail, like a movie reel, and yeah, it was sweet...until I got to the credits. "They'll know it was us, Sketch. No way Pete would let it go. I know him. He's my best fr—" Who was I kidding? I didn't have a best friend anymore.

"Jesus, Jonathan! That's why I've been telling you we need a Gay-Straight Alliance here! An organization that tells everyone in this stupid, bigoted school that we are here and will not accept treatment like this. C'mon! Talk to Principal Hardin with us!" Sketch paced around the art room. She'd been making this argument for over a week, but I was still unconvinced.

"I don't think it solves anything to make ourselves more visible," I said for the hundredth time.

"You seriously need to grow a pair!" She glared at me.

"Sketch, stop. He's right." Mason brushed an eraser-shaped chalk mark off his pants. "Don't get me wrong, I'm all for it. Itching powder in their jockstraps. Photographic proof of a scratch fest gone bad. Pete, Luke, Brandon humiliated in front of the whole school"—he stopped fiddling with his pants— "but you were right, much as it kills me to admit it. I lied and told people you were my girlfriend two years ago because I wasn't ready to have everyone up in my business, judging me. We take this fight to Pete and we confirm everything Luke is saying about Jonathan, and I won't let him be outed like that." His clenched his jaw. "No, what we need to do, and fast, is come up with a plan for damage control. Specifically, we need to figure out who is going to walk him to classes today."

"I do not need to be walked to classes!" I objected, despite the fact that he'd just blown me away.

"Trust me, you do." Mason's voice dropped a few levels. His eyes looked past me. Or maybe they just looked into the past.

"Okay, but I'm going to buy some itching powder after school today in case either of you eunuchs decide that you've had enough and want to stand up to them. In the meantime, Jonathan, Mason can walk you to classes this morning. We'll all go through the lunch line together, and I'll walk with you this afternoon."

The first hour warning bell rang. Sketch took the tarp off her *Dying Dove* canvas, and I found myself staring at it. The protruding bone. The dripping blood. The feeling of being under fire.

Mason followed my gaze. "You want to know how the dove lives? By saying nothing. Not one word. By keeping his head up and looking 'em in the eye and moving right past them like they're invisible. You understand?" Mason asked as Ms. Owens and other students streamed into class.

I nodded, picked up my camera, and flicked through the various settings, wondering what speed and aperture would make my world come back into focus. For once, my Nikon failed me.

CHAPTER NINE

"Pete, over here!" I shouted during practice after school. Coach was running a scrimmage with us divided into two teams. Lucky me, I was on the same team with Pete. Not that it made much difference. Everyone had seen the picture.

Pete was trapped in the midfield, surrounded by Zack and Austin, keeping the ball alive by kicking it between his feet while he scanned for a decent pass.

He glanced at me where I stood with nothing but green between me and the goal, planted his foot, and took aim for Brandon. Dumbass. Luke had Brandon covered. Pete kicked, sending the ball toward Brandon, and just as I expected, Luke intercepted.

"What the hell, Pete?" Ethan shouted. "Jonathan was wide open. Are you blind?"

Pete flipped Ethan off and glared at me. Like it was somehow my fault.

Coach Thomas blew the whistle and called us over, presumably for an ass-chewing. I walked over to the circle and heard it—Brandon whispering, "Jesus, why doesn't he get a clue and quit already?"

I kept my head up, looked him in the eye, and walked right past him. He might as well have been invisible.

Ethan looked at me and smiled. It wasn't much, but it was enough.

❖

"Where's Mason?" I found Sketch sitting on the concrete floor outside the boys' locker room after practice. The sour scent of sweat hung in the air.

"*Project Runway* finale on Bravo. He probably sprinted all the way home."

I laughed and sat on the floor beside her. "So, are you waiting to assault some unsuspecting jockstraps with itching powder after everyone leaves? Because I should warn you, they're pretty ripe."

"Gross!" Sketch crinkled her nose. "And no, I drew parking lot duty."

I exhaled. "Look, this whole *we need to babysit Jonathan* routine has to stop."

Sketch nodded. "Couldn't agree more. Let's go talk to Principal Hardin."

I stared at the patch of wall between the boys' locker room and the equipment storage closet where our team name sprawled in faded blue and dingy white. And I remembered that moment at camp when I'd faced the storm—the one that raged outside and the one inside me—and I hadn't given a damn what anyone would think, but that had been camp. This was *my school, my team, my home*. I shook my head. "Don't you get it, Sketch? Starting a GSA confirms every rumor. I'm no crusader."

She touched my arm, and I looked at her. "For the record, Jonathan, lots of straight people join a GSA simply because they believe everyone has the right to go to a safe school. Everyone will assume you're an ally."

"You don't really believe that."

"Actually, I do. Mason and I talked about it after school. He's been feeling people out today. Turns out almost everyone thinks Luke and Pete are jerks and that a picture of you swimming proves nothing. Jesus, I've been breathing in the testosterone pheromones down here for, like, an hour and a half. I've probably lost about twenty IQ points. But I couldn't wait to tell you the news. What took you so long?"

"Coach made me stay late to practice some new defense strategies."

"Not a moment too soon."

"I thought you said their text was a bust."

"Jonathan, I hate to break it to you, but I doubt Pete and Luke are done with you. You've got to be ready for their next move. I wonder..." Sketch studied my face, then looked away.

"What?" I asked.

"I'm just trying to decide something."

"Which is..."

"Whether you're ready or not. I think you are. I'm just not completely sure."

"Let me know what you decide." I stood to leave. I'd had enough of people judging me for one day.

"Wait, let me ask you a question, and give me an honest answer, okay?"

I slung my backpack over my shoulder. "I'd turn the wallet in. Can I go now?"

Sketch grinned at me. "Why do you think the dove lives?"

The question hung there, suspended in the pheromone-filled air while I thought about it.

"Because you aren't just painting what it feels like to be under fire."

"I'm not?" She looked offended. "Then what am I painting, Picasso?"

"You're painting," I said, remembering how she'd feathered a touch of rose along the bloody gash, "what it feels like to survive and begin to heal."

Sketch nodded and stood beside me. "Okay, let's go."

I looked at my watch. 4:30 p.m. "Where?"

"Does it matter?"

"Not at all," I said as we walked down the hallway. "But I have to be home by 5:45."

"So close, Jonathan. You should have stopped at *not at all*."

Outside, the wind tasted of fall and freedom. I grew lighter, step after step, as we walked three blocks from school. The leaves on the trees that lined the streets looked like Sketch had attacked them with her paintbrush, a beautiful mosaic of gold and crimson filtering the light. I followed her into the covered bus shelter.

"We're taking a bus?" I asked as the 6B Metro transit pulled into view.

"No, we are taking the TARDIS."

"The what?"

"The TARDIS. Or don't you watch *Doctor Who*?" The look on her face said I better come up with the right answer.

"It isn't blue," I pointed out.

"Good. You are not as hopeless as I thought. This, my friend, is the American version of the TARDIS."

I thought about telling her that comparing real life to a science fiction show might have caused her expulsion from the cool group, but then I figured she already knew that and didn't care. "Let me guess, in this little scenario, you're the Doctor," I said, which earned a snort-laugh from Sketch.

"No, but I am going to introduce you to him, and

together we're going to show you how to take control of your universe."

"Great. As long as we can do it in an hour."

The door of the bus/American version of the TARDIS (which really was much bigger inside than it looked) opened for us, and we boarded. I still had no clue where we were going.

Thirty minutes later, we pulled up to the bus stop on Hennepin Avenue, the heart of downtown Minneapolis. I stepped off and looked around for some clue to where Sketch was taking me. She looped her arm through mine and pulled me past a ginormous cherry that perched on top of an even more ginormous spoon. For a minute, I almost believed her TARDIS theory, but then we walked past a sign that read Minneapolis Sculpture Garden. She led me to a large, square gray building I assumed was the Walker Art Center, and I stood there, my chest tightening as I remembered the promise I'd made to Ian.

I was supposed to come here with him.

"Hello! Earth to Jonathan." She snapped her fingers in front of my face. "You with me?"

"Yeah, I'm with you," I said, following her into a very large, very white, very sparkly room.

"Well, I'll be! Francie has come for a visit, and she's brought a handsome young man with her. Did you see that, Enid? It's your Francie with a *young man*!" An old man wheezed and pointed at us from behind the information table. Next to him sat an equally old woman with sparkling black eyes the exact shade of Sketch's. Her gray hair stood out in spikes and swirls. Enid sprang up from behind the table and scooted over to us. She was tiny. And bouncy. She hopped up and down, words flying from her lips in every direction, hitting everyone with equal force.

"Hush, Ray. You know my Francie likes to be called Sketch. 'Cuz she's an artist. It runs in the family. You show her some respect and call her what she likes to be called! A young girl doesn't have enough freedom of choice in this world as it is. Now come here and give me a kiss!" she said, thankfully talking to Sketch. "It's been too long. You should be ashamed. Not coming to see old Ray and me, though I know your mother doesn't approve, but she is a fool. Choosing books over art! Lord help me, I raised a fool. And you"—she turned to examine me—"let me look at you. Nice young man. Isn't he a nice young man, Ray? My Francie has found herself, whoops, 'scuse me, my Sketch has found herself a nice young man. Now give me a hug." She wrapped her arms around my waist since that was all she could reach and squeezed with surprising strength.

"Hi, Grams. This is Jonathan. He's a photographer." Sketch leaned her head on my shoulder, which sent Enid into spasms. I put my arm around Sketch's waist because Enid's joy was contagious in a good way.

"Your name is Francie?" I whispered.

Sketch jabbed me in the ribs with her elbow. "Shut up. It's Frances, but if you call me that again, I'll aim lower next time." Louder (much louder because she was talking to Enid) she said, "Okay if I show Jonathan around?"

"Of course, but if anyone in a blue blazer asks, you paid for your passes!" Enid handed us two orange tags, and we clipped them to our shirts. With Ray's advice not to get caught smooching in the dark corners, we went in search of *how to take control of my universe.*

The Walker was filled with paintings and statues and hidden rooms and things that didn't look like art at all but made me feel something, which Sketch told me made them art. I found myself wondering what else she knew that I didn't.

"Quit looking at your watch! You'll never learn a damn thing if you're worried about being late for dinner." It was the third time Sketch scolded me in an hour, but she didn't know my mother. "Besides, we're here!" She pulled me around a corner and pointed at a black-and-white photo that hung on the far wall. *That's it? You brought me here to see a small photograph? Because that hidden room was way cooler,* I thought at first glance. The image became clearer as we walked closer. My chest tightened. I forgot how to breathe as I stared at the placard beside the picture. *Two Men Dancing,* by Robert Mapplethorpe, 1984. Chest to chest, skin touching, they danced. I sucked in a deep breath, feeling everything as I studied the picture. That hand on the back! The head on the shoulder, dark—not red, but excruciatingly familiar. And the crowns on top of both their heads? Impossible! I took a step closer, searching their faces, looking for what I knew had to be there, but wasn't. *Where?* I wanted to yell at them. *Where is your shame?* They answered me with peace and love, which made me want to yell even more.

I turned to walk away, but Sketch grabbed my arm and wouldn't let me.

"Where are you're going? This is why I brought you here."

"Why? To show me a lie?"

"You only think that because—"

I was suddenly sick of being Sketch's art student/project/pity case. "You don't get it, do you? People like me don't get to dance with the people we love, much less wear a crown!" My voice rose. The docent in the corner shot a warning glance at me.

"They do if they take control of their universe!" Sketch argued.

"This isn't a stupid sci-fi show, Sketch. There is no

TARDIS, and nobody gets to go back in time and fix things," I whisper-shouted, spraying her face. I would have turned away from me, but she didn't.

"Don't you get it, Jonathan? *You* are the Doctor in your universe! You've got the power to take control of your life! I brought you here so you could see this picture and know that it's okay to be yourself, wear your crown, hold your head high and be proud! That's what a GSA is all about. Refusing to be ashamed of who you are. Refusing to think that somehow you deserve what those assholes are doing to you."

The pain that had been building since I got home from camp surfaced and lodged in my throat. Tears burned in my eyes. I turned away from Sketch, but not before she saw my face.

"Go ahead, Jonathan. Cry."

"I don't want to cry. I want to yell."

"Then yell! Robert Mapplethorpe would approve."

But I couldn't.

Not in the middle of the gallery with a middle-aged couple mingling nearby. Not with the supervising docent who was already frowning at us.

"C'mon, Jonathan! Let it out!"

"Why won't you leave me alone? I don't want to *let it out* or put itching powder in my friends' jockstraps or join your stupid GSA!" I turned to walk away, but she grabbed me. "Let me *go*!" I wrenched my arm out of her grasp.

She took a step back. Hurt flooded her face. She turned her back on me and stared at the Mapplethorpe picture, her shoulders shaking, and I knew I'd gone too far.

"Sketch, look, I'm sorry," I whispered. "I didn't mean to say those things."

She sighed. "Which is different than saying you didn't mean those things."

"I'm just not ready."

"I know. It's okay."

I could have handled her telling me to fuck off. I could have handled her walking out on me. But understanding? That broke me.

Sketch pulled a brown Taco John napkin from her backpack and gave it to me. I sopped up as best I could.

"Why?" I asked when I'd recovered the minimum amount of dignity needed to talk.

"Because those guys? Pete, Brandon, Luke? They aren't your friends. You just think they are." She leaned her head on my shoulder, not for show or for Enid. This time it was real. I rested my head on hers and hoped I was done dripping. Friends deserved better treatment than to have snot land on them. Especially real friends.

CHAPTER TEN

In a lot of ways, life got better after that day at the museum. My ankle healed. I hit 501 push-ups one morning, breaking Dad's record. My biceps bulged in places they'd never bulged before. Plus, I had a spot to sit at lunch. I even had people to sit with, and I didn't miss my view of the lake…much. I couldn't stop thinking about *Two Men Dancing* and spent hours searching the Internet for anything about Robert Mapplethorpe and his work. A lot of it shocked me, and I was pretty sure I knew why he had not made Ms. Owens's list of photographers to study. Art critics called him brilliant. My mother would have called him obscene. I called him confusing. It wasn't so much the nudity in his work. It was the attitude he captured in every picture. *I am a man. See my boner. I am gay.* Over and over, picture after picture, Robert Mapplethorpe didn't ask permission or offer an apology. I envied him. The guy had real balls. I'd seen them. Then I read that Robert Mapplethorpe died at the age of forty-two from complications arising from AIDS, and I didn't envy him so much after that. But still I searched for details about his life long into the night. I printed out his pictures and snuck them into the art room where, with Mason keeping an eye out for Ms. Owens, I studied his use of light and shadow. I marveled that his first work had been done with a Polaroid. Impossible, but true. I felt inept on so many levels. On the plus side, I discovered a way to respond to Ian's sexting. He'd sext me, and I'd send him one of Mapplethorpe's pictures. Ian constantly complained that the only culture he experienced on the farm turned milk to cheese. Sharing Robert Mapplethorpe with him was the least I could do.

But in some ways, life got worse. It was the second Friday in October, two weeks from the homecoming game against Sacred Heart. I'd gotten used to playing defense on the field or in the locker room, but in the cafeteria? That seemed out of bounds, even for Pete.

Mason, Sketch, and I were sitting in lunch one day when a freshman walked up to our table, holding out a banana for me.

"Pete Mitchell told me to give this to you, Jonathan. He said you had a special use for it. Whatever that's supposed to mean," the freshman said, and I accepted it because I didn't want the poor kid to get in trouble with Pete. Mason took a huge bite of pizza and grunted something that sounded suspiciously like *Don't be a wimp, Dick,* though it could have been limp. Who knows? The kid's name could have been Dick.

"A midterm exam on *The Scarlet Letter* on Monday? Goddamn, Gilchrist. I bet he spends his night plotting how to ruin perfectly good weekends." Mason slapped his palm on the table and glared.

"We're all in American lit. Why don't we get together on Saturday and study?" I suggested.

Mason scowled some more, but Sketch nodded. "Good idea. Do you suppose Gilchrist would notice if we had the same answer to every question? The guy's, what? A hundred years old?"

"At least!" Mason said.

"Pretty sure he'd notice." I peeled the banana and took a bite. Shrieks of laughter and the sound of fist pounding from Pete's table erupted in the lunchroom. Face burning, I tossed the banana in the nearest garbage can.

"For Christ's sake, Jonathan!" Sketch shook her head. "Do you have to make it so easy for them?"

I didn't answer her, except to say, "So, are we meeting this weekend or what?" Mason grunted, which I took to mean yes. Sketch nodded. "Next question then. Where?"

"Not my house. My mom's throwing a baby shower for my sister on Saturday, and she'd pitch a fit if I had company over." Mason rolled his eyes. "We might walk on the carpet or touch something! God forbid!"

"What about your place?" I asked Sketch, but she frowned and stared out the window.

"No can do. Mom is prepping for a big case on Monday." The tone of her voice did not leave room for discussion.

"Okay, my place it is then. Ten a.m. okay?"

"Are you crazy? I cannot function before noon!" Mason protested. I thought about pointing out that half his classes occurred before noon, but decided against it. Other than Sketch, he was the only friend I had at school.

"Noon it is," I said just as the bell rang.

❖

Sketch showed up at my door with six boxes of Junior Mints, three two-liters of Mountain Dew, and season one of *Doctor Who*.

"What? The brain runs on glucose. I came prepared," she said after I gave her crap about bringing enough sugar to put us all into a diabetic coma.

"And *Doctor Who*?"

"We have to take a break sometime. We might as well spend it inside the TARDIS," Sketch said.

I was about to remind her that we were supposed to be studying when Mom walked into the living room.

Her eyes widened as they traveled over the chains on Sketch's torn jeans, her spiked wristband. I thought she was going to faint when she noticed the fishnet nylons that poked out from the huge chunk of missing material that should have been covering Sketch's left butt cheek. "I didn't know we were having company today."

I recognized Mom's tone, though I doubted Sketch would. Most people didn't pick up on the undercurrents that ran beneath the surface of Mom's polite exterior. "This is Sketch, Mom. We're studying for Gilchrist's midterm."

"Sketch?" Mom's eyebrows disappeared beneath her bangs. "And don't you mean *Mr.* Gilchrist, Jonathan?" The doorbell rang again, sparing me from answering.

I opened the door and found myself staring into a bulging brown bag.

"Thought we might get hungry." Mason's voice came from behind the bag. "I made salsa with fresh lime and cilantro. Also, red pepper hummus and oven-baked pita chips seasoned with garlic-infused olive oil."

"Hot damn! Way to go, Mason!" Sketch exclaimed from behind me.

I turned to look at my mom, but she had disappeared, no doubt in a funk because Sketch had said the word *damn* in her living room. "Consider that *hot damn* seconded." I smiled and led them into the kitchen.

"Wow." Sketch blinked. "That is the brightest yellow I've ever seen."

"Holy Dolce and Gabbana!" Mason shielded his eyes with his hand. "You should have a basket of sunglasses sitting on the counter."

"Exactly, because some poor, unsuspecting visitor could walk in here and have a seizure triggered. You'd be liable, you know," Sketch added.

Mason and I laughed and grabbed the plates and glasses from the cupboard.

I led them up the stairs to my bedroom where Butler sprawled in a patch of light. "Meet Butler, the world's youngest fifteen-year-old cat."

"You painted your cat yellow too?" Mason flopped on my bed. "I think it's time for an intervention. Sketch, you, as a serious canvas artist, should lead it. There must be a twelve-step program or something."

"There is." Sketch sat on my desk chair and spun in a circle. "Jonathan, repeat after me, I am powerless over the color yellow…"

Over the course of the afternoon, each of us consumed approximately 4,753 calories, most of them from high fructose corn syrup. Sketch watched six straight episodes of *Doctor Who* on my Mac while she picked chunks of dried paint out of Butler's fur, earning her numerous scratches and bite marks. I spent the afternoon laughing at Mason, who wrote twelve affirmations for a program he named YAA, Yellow Addicts Anonymous. I stopped listening when he crashed on my bed and recited them to David Beckham in a British accent. What we didn't do was study for the midterm on *The Scarlet Letter*.

Mom's voice came through the door in the middle of the seventh episode of *Doctor Who*. "Are your guests staying for dinner, Jonathan? Because I'll have to run to the grocery store if they are."

Sketch and Mason correctly interpreted this to mean *Are they ever going to leave?* and began collecting the empty chip and cookie bags, leaving the crumbs for Butler to feast on.

"They're getting ready to go now," I assured Mom, shrugging an apology.

"No offense, but your mom is a little high-strung," Sketch said once the sound of my mother's footsteps receded.

"You don't know the half of it," I said and wrestled a garlic-infused oven-baked pita chip out of Butler's mouth.

Later that night, just when all the questions on *The Scarlet Letter* study guide began to blur, I heard the ping of a text. It was Ian, griping about his homework.

Shit, I hate midterms. I had to write a paper for history today. What are you doing?

Studying for an exam. Well, sort of. What's the paper on? I texted.

He replied right away. *A military figure who abused his power. It was a tossup between Attila the Hun and Fidel Castro. Chose Attila when I found out that some people think he croaked from a hemorrhoid in his esophagus. Guess what?*

What? I asked him.

I'm never gonna look at Matilda's double chin the same way ever again.

I laughed, and later, when I lay in my bed, I promised David Beckham that Mason was a decent enough guy despite the whole YAA in a British accent thing. Leg pulled back and face screwed up in a frown, David looked doubtful so I told him that maybe, just maybe, there could be such a thing as life beyond soccer after all.

And when he *really* didn't buy that, I pulled out the pictures of him in his underwear and we had a completely different type of conversation.

CHAPTER ELEVEN

Sunday mornings in the fall at the Cooper household meant three things: 8:30 a.m. church at Redeemer Southern Baptist, brunch at Maynard's, and (when Dad was home) football on the television. Most Sundays it was fine. Tolerable even. Except for the Sunday after Sketch and Mason's visit when Pete and his family sat in the row in front of us in church. The pit in my stomach mushroomed into a boulder when Mom leaned forward and tapped Pete on the shoulder.

"I haven't seen you in ages, Peter. Why haven't you come over to the house? Of course, I know you boys are busy with soccer season, but maybe you could have another sleepover like you used to."

Pete turned around and stared at me. "Thanks, Mrs. Cooper, but we're a little old for sleepovers. Right, Jonathan?" He clenched his jaw.

"Right." I swallowed and then a small miracle occurred. Pastor Jim started the service and my mother had to shut up. The sermon was about the good shepherd and the lost sheep, and I found myself wondering whether the sheep had wandered off or run away.

I wanted to go home after church, but no, Mom took up residence in the fellowship hall, sipping coffee and talking

Sunday school curriculum. When she started showing paint swatches to her cronies, I knew she had settled in for the long haul, and I wandered into the empty sanctuary. The room was quiet. Too quiet. I couldn't help but think about my life as I stared at the large wooden cross that hung from the ceiling above the altar.

"Lord, I'm confused." My thoughts traveled back to the shore of Spirit Lake. To the first time I'd admitted my feelings for Ian to my favorite counselor. It seemed like a lifetime ago. "Simon says you love me just as I am. If that's true, God, why do I feel like I don't belong here anymore?" My words hung in the air with the smoke from the blown out candles. Stale and motionless. I left the sanctuary in search of relief of a different variety.

I swung open the door of the men's bathroom.

"What the fuck? Get out of here!" Pete screamed and shoved his body even farther into the urinal.

Sometimes you charge. Sometimes you retreat. A smart soldier knows when to do which, my father always said, but this time I listened to my bladder.

"Get over yourself." I picked the stall farthest away from Pete and let it fly. In retrospect, I should have listened to my father.

My kidneys had just begun to thank me when the right one took the punch. My knees buckled, and I found myself, eye level with the urinal cake, piss splashing onto my pants and the floor. Pete grabbed my arm and twisted it behind my back. He put his hand on my head and shoved it toward the urinal and the white disk that sat in the drain. I had just enough time to wonder why anyone would name such a gross thing a cake when Pete shoved my head inside the urinal and I eliminated taste as a reason.

"What the hell?" I struggled and shouted though it came

out garbled since my mouth was pressed against the urinal-distinctly-not-cake. "Leave me alone!"

"Listen up!" Pete panted into my right ear, his hand shoving my face even farther into the pool of warm urine. "You think you've got everyone fooled? Walking around at school like everyone doesn't know exactly what you are? Fine, keep thinking that, but don't you ever walk in on me in a bathroom again! Not here and not at school or you'll wish you never lived. Do you understand that, Cooper? You use the girls' bathroom where you belong!"

I grunted, I think. I'm not really sure because whatever sound I produced was quickly drowned in the spray of water and the sucking gurgle as Pete flushed the urinal.

"Why?" I managed to say when he let go of me and I sank to the bathroom floor. "Is it because of...you know? Because I've never told anyone!"

He washed his hands in the sink and dried them with a paper towel, slow and deliberate, and tossed it into the garbage. "I don't know what you're talking about." He held his head high, stared straight ahead, and walked out the door.

Mom was mid-story in the fellowship hall, which meant less than shit to me at the moment.

"I'm leaving. Now."

Shock registered on her face. Her coffee cup shook in her hand. The cronies around the table gaped at me and the dark stain that covered the front of my khaki pants.

"I'll walk if I have to."

"Excuse me, ladies." She stood, her eyes darting over their faces.

"Yeah, they're looking at me. Can we go now?" I stormed off toward the coatroom. She caught up with me just as I pulled my coat off the hanger.

"What happened, Jonathan? Why are you soaking wet?"

I wanted to tell her, but it seemed that I'd swallowed the words for so long that I couldn't speak them so I said nothing and headed for the front door.

"Jonathan, you will tell me this instant what happened to you!" Her voice turned into a shriek the moment we stepped outside the church, the October wind biting our faces. It was a convenient fact that no one was around to hear her.

Nope. I still couldn't tell her.

"Fine. Don't talk to me. But I am going to talk with your father if I have to call the Pentagon myself. I can't deal with this on my own any longer!" She yanked the car door open and slid into the driver's seat. She started the car, her hands shaking as she reached to turn on the heat. I closed my eyes, not needing to watch the streets fly by as we made our way home. I already knew where we were heading.

"We are not done talking about this!" She yelled at me again as I slammed the house door and headed toward the stairs that led to the second story.

"I have homework to do."

Her response, if she had any, never made it through my closed bedroom door, but I knew what she was doing. Calling everyone she knew at the marine base, trying to figure out how to track down Dad.

I tried to study, but I couldn't focus. I pulled out my cell and sent a text.

Hey, you there? Can I call you? I really need to talk to you.

He replied a few seconds later.

Yeah, but I'm currently getting my ass chewed.

What for? I texted.

Same old, same old.

I knew what that meant. Ian had been fighting. Again. Most

of the time I envied how he stood up for himself. Sometimes, like now, it just made me feel like a wuss.

I started another text. This time to Sketch.

Okay, you've got your—

"Jonathan, are you all right?" Mom barged into my room without knocking.

"Hey! How about some privacy?" I gripped my cell in my fist.

"Excuse me? The last time I checked, your father and I pay the mortgage on this house."

This from the woman who had been showing her cronies paint swatches in the fellowship hall while Pete was shoving my head in a urinal? Seriously? "What do you want?

"You're not acting like yourself at all." She crossed the room and put her hand on my forehead.

I yanked away and glared at her. "Did you reach him?" Which really meant *does he know about me and, OMG, what did he say?*

She shook her head. "I talked with his sergeant major. He'll try to get a message to your father's unit, but they're in transit to Afghanistan right now." She reached for my forehead again.

I pulled away from her. "Read. My. Lips. I'm *not* sick! Why can't you just leave me alone?" She flinched and walked out of the room, slamming my door to make her point.

I pulled out my phone and finished the text.

Okay, you've got your third. I hit send.

Maybe, I thought, Mr. Gilchrist will come down with a bad case of swine flu and he won't be at school tomorrow. Maybe, when Dad calls, Mom will forget to tell him about what happened this summer. Maybe Pete will choke on a banana overnight or, better yet, a urinal cake.

Sketch's text arrived a few minutes later.

What did Pete do now?

I had to hand it to her. She didn't waste time with bullshit. I hit the reply button. *What are you talking about?*

She responded right away. *Something made you change your mind. What was it?*

You want a third or what? I texted.

I want you to be okay more.

Too late for that! I wanted to tell her, looking at the spot on my bedroom floor where it had happened so long ago, these things I was paying for now. *I am anything but okay.*

It had been dark in my bedroom. Long shadows had crept across the floor littered with still bodies, gangly legs and arms poking out of sleeping bags in awkward angles.

The sugar buzz had worn off somewhere around midnight, but we had kept going on the fumes of friendship, laughing into the early morning when they had finally fallen asleep. Brandon and Ethan and Zack and Austin. Their whispers and giggles had died away into the sound of deep breathing.

The floor, like me, had grown harder by the minute as I lay there, waiting for the sound I knew would come.

The rustle of his sleeping bag next to me. It was a god-awful thing. Lime green on the inside with stupid space robots and cowboys with twirling ropes on the outside. A kid's sleeping bag really, but that's not why we had laughed about it the summer between sixth and seventh grade. We had laughed because a lot of things had changed. For one, Pete had shot up three inches over the winter, and even when he scrunched down inside it, the sleeping bag barely covered his nipples. For another, the words *Buzz* and *Woody* had taken on new meanings for all of us.

But some things hadn't changed. Not since the sleepover in fifth grade when Brandon had bragged that his was the biggest so of course all of us had challenged him. Maybe he'd said the longest. I don't remember. I don't even remember whose had been the biggest or the longest, but I do remember what happened later, and what had happened at every sleepover afterward until we grew too old for sleepovers and everything took on a new meaning.

I'm fine, I texted Sketch.

CHAPTER TWELVE

I crack open my eyes and spot Grace slumped in a chair by my bedside. Her thin arms cross in front of her body. Her head droops to one side, and her lips flutter in and out, producing a small whiffling sound that holds me to this place. Hours have passed, but the light inside the room has not changed. Warm and white, it comes up from the floor, down from the ceiling, off the walls.

"Who is Ian?" Grace asks, and I wonder if she's been awake this whole time.

"He's my…my…" I pull Ian toward me. He rests his head on my shoulder. I place one hand on his back. Raise the other for him to hold. Around and around, we move to music only we can hear. I try to sit up. Try to hum the song so she can hear it and understand, but beeping and buzzing scatters the music. A blur of red light swirls around my bed.

"I want the truth from him!" I hear his voice in the hallway, the blotch of blue. A burst of light flashes in my eyes, and I open my mouth, but the light swallows the sound of me yelling.

Grace leans over my bed and grabs my hands, holds them tight as can be. "You stay with me, Jonathan Cooper. It's too early for any of that." The spinning stops, and I find myself settling into one fixed place again.

"I'm not going away until I talk to him!" The voice is distant, muffled.

"You know damn well that you are not allowed in this room while I am here!" Grace glares, and I imagine the heat from her eyes burning through the wooden door, finishing him off once and for all. It's a nice dream, but a dream nonetheless.

"I don't know what to tell him." The music notes return and float suspended in the air. I reach out my hand, but they dance away.

"That's what you and I are trying to figure out." Grace starts to hum.

"You know this song?" I ask and she smiles, so wide I can see her dentures shift in her mouth.

"Of course I do, Jonathan. Everyone does. We're born knowing it, but somewhere along the journey most people forget." She leans back in the chair and closes her eyes. Starts to hum again. Soft and lilting, the music weaves around me like a blanket.

CHAPTER THIRTEEN

I think we should ask Ms. Owens." Sketch walked over to the red light district where Mason and I were dinking around on the computers. It was Monday morning. The midterm exam was looming, but that was the last thing on Sketch's mind.

"All right, everyone. Pick up your brush or camera. I think we're ready to start!" Ms. Owens had been arranging gourds on a table for the past ten minutes. The words were barely out of her mouth when one of the gourds rolled off the table. "No, not again!" She knelt to pick one off the floor.

"Okay, but let's wait 'til after class," I said.

"Fine." Sketch harrumphed. "What about Ms. Jennings? She took a stand on evolution a few years ago."

"Definitely," Mason said. "And also Mr. Gilchrist."

I thought about it. "I guess it couldn't hurt to ask."

"Quickly, everyone! Grab your medium of choice and let's begin!" Ms. Owens interrupted any further discussion.

❖

"Now." Sketch stuck her brush in a jar of turpentine and walked toward Ms. Owens, who was guarding the table with the stacked gourds that had, miraculously, made it through the hour without rolling away again. Mason and I trailed behind her.

"Ms. Owens, could I ask you a question?"

"Of course, Sketch. Just don't bump the table. I need these gourds for one more hour."

We stopped a few feet away. "Mason, Jonathan, and I want to start a new club at school. Principal Hardin said we needed to have three students and an advisor. We've got the three of us, and we were hoping you would be the advisor."

"An art club? That's a wonderful idea!" Ms. Owens leaned against the table, sending the gourds in every direction.

"No, not an art club. A GSA actually." Sketch grabbed a gourd as it rolled off the edge of the table.

"A GSA? What kind of a club is that?" Ms. Owens had a gourd in each hand. Mason and I picked up the ones from the floor and put them on the table where she began constructing her gourd masterpiece again.

"GSA. It stands for Gay-Straight Alliance." I had to admire Sketch. She didn't blink or flinch as she said the words. Ms. Owen's hand froze midair.

"Oh my, of course I'm supportive. I mean, some people think that Michelangelo and Da Vinci were, and of course, there's that sweet boy, Doogie Howser."

Beside me, Mason choked. Sketch sighed. "And lots of other people, Ms. Owens. Approximately ten percent of the population identifies as gay, lesbian, bisexual, transgendered, or questioning. That means in your average class of thirty students, you are probably teaching three GLBTQ students every hour."

Ms. Owens stopped stacking gourds and looked at Mason, Sketch, and me. "Three? Really? What a coincidence. I would love to help you. I would, but a GSA at East Bay Christian

Academy? That would mean Principal Hardin and the board of trustees, and…oh my, I'm just not sure it's advisable."

The color drained from Sketch's face. Her lips tightened.

"It is if we find a teacher who cares more about keeping her students safe than she does about keeping her job." Sketch hip-checked the table and walked out, leaving Ms. Owens to chase her gourds.

The bell had already rung, so it was a foregone conclusion that we were all going to be late to second hour. Rushing seemed pointless.

"You were a little harsh on her, don't you think?" I asked Sketch who fumed as she stomped down the hallway.

"Harsh? She as much as told us that her job is more important than we are."

"Think about it, Sketch. This is a private school, which means no tenure and no union protecting the teachers. Hardin could fire Ms. Owens for advising a GSA and he wouldn't even have to give a reason."

"That's irrelevant."

"Not to Ms. Owens, it's not."

Mason and I had to leave Sketch to think about that when we reached the American lit classroom. Mr. Gilchrist, who showed no symptoms of swine flu or any other test-giving-debilitating disease, passed out the exams. I groaned. I still had ten chapters of *The Scarlet Letter* left to read.

Question number one: Describe the role of the people of Salem who watched Hester's punishment play out every day and did nothing. What does this imply about their strength of character? About their views of right and wrong?

At least Gilchrist was asking for a hypothetical answer, which meant the only way to get it wrong was to say Hester Prynne built a rocket ship and flew to the moon or something. I argued that the villagers had weak characters since they should have stood up for Hester instead of passively participating in her persecution. I felt like a big hypocrite since I hadn't even read a third of the book. But still, it was an argument I could get behind.

Mason finished before I did and brought his exam to Mr. Gilchrist who sat behind his desk, drinking coffee.

"Mr. Gilchrist, I wanted to ask you a question." Mason's voice carried throughout the hushed test-taking room. I stared, unable to believe Mason was a) brave enough, and b) stupid enough to bring it up at the worst possible moment. I slunk down in my chair and concentrated on essay question number ten.

"Certainly. How can I help you?" Mr. Gilchrist peered over his coffee cup at Mason.

"Sketch Mallory, Jonathan Cooper, and I are trying to form a Gay-Straight Alliance, but we need an advisor to oversee our club. I was wondering if you would help us out?" He lowered his voice when it came to the actual question, but I heard him. In fact, everyone heard him. They even heard Mr. Gilchrist choke on his coffee.

"Take on the role of advisor to a Gay-Straight Alliance?" Mr. Gilchrist clutched his coffee cup in his hand. "I'm afraid that's unthinkable."

"Why is it unthinkable?" Mason pushed. If looks could have killed him, I'd be on trial for murder.

Mr. Gilchrist's hand trembled as he put the cup on his desk. "Do I need to remind you what school you are attending, Mr. Kellerman?"

"No, sir, you don't. It's always been my understanding that East Bay Christian Academy was founded in memory of a young man who died trying to fight oppression. Given the chance, I like to think that Lieutenant Lance Porter would have fought to keep all the students of this school safe. Not just the straight ones."

For once, Mr. Gilchrist was speechless. Mason, though defeated, had made an important point, and everyone in American lit, including Pete, had heard him.

Mason, Sketch, and I tallied up the nos at lunch.

"It was a bust with Gilchrist," Mason said.

Sketch nodded. "I expected that. Ms. Jennings also said no."

"Get out of here!" I put down my fork and stared at her. Ms. Jennings, *Evolution Champion and Board of Trustees Swayer,* had said no? "Well then, it's hopeless, Sketch. You might as well face the fact that no teacher in this school is going to advise a Gay-Straight Alliance. It's time to give up."

Sketch crushed her empty milk carton. "I will not! This school needs a GSA, and you, more than anyone, know that."

Mason cleared his throat. "I think what Jonathan is trying to say is that we're dead in the water without an advisor."

"Thank you for interpreting Jonathan's statement for me." Sketch sneered. "But we're not out of options yet. Jonathan, I think you should ask Coach Thomas."

"No. Absolutely not. I refuse."

"C'mon, this is your chance to be the Doctor and take control of your universe!"

"Sketch." I chose my words carefully so that there could be no doubt left in her one-track mind. "I would rather be attacked by a million Daleks."

At least Mason laughed.

Chapter Fourteen

M om made broccoli cheese casserole for dinner that night. We ate at the small table in the kitchen like we always did when Dad was gone. I pushed the soggy mess around the yellow and blue Fiesta plates Mom had bought to match the kitchen.

That was when she broke the news. "I made an appointment for us to see Pastor Jim after school on Thursday."

"You did what?" I plopped a spoonful of sour cream on the concoction, even though the god-awful taste that flooded my mouth had nothing to do with her cooking. "This is because of Ian, isn't it?" I shoved a bite in my mouth.

Sadly, the sour cream did not help.

She sighed. "Jonathan, you're young, and you're confused. You just think you have feelings for that boy."

"I don't *think* I have feelings for Ian, Mom. I *have* feelings for Ian, and I am *not* confused! I know who I am even if you don't! I'm g—"

"Don't say that!" She cringed. "Don't say that to anyone!"

I'd had enough. "Sketch, Mason, and I are starting a Gay-Straight Alliance at school. I thought you should know."

Dinner got real quiet real fast after that.

I finished eating in three bites, not caring anymore about how anything tasted. "May I be excused?"

"No, we're not done discussing this." She crossed the room and poured herself a cup of coffee. I flinched. Chats that required caffeine after dinner were never good.

"I've got a lot of homework. Can't this wait?"

"No, it can't. I spoke with your father today. We both agree that Pastor Jim might be able to help you with…all of this."

"Dad called?" My pulse jumped in my throat. "He knows?"

She nodded. "He called while you were at school. I told him about everything that happened last summer. What's happening now." She poured cream into her cup as if that could somehow sweeten things.

"So the two of you think I'm so messed up I need to go to Christian counseling with Pastor Jim?"

"No, Jonathan, we love you. You know that." She leaned against the counter, her thin shoulders sagging. "Do you remember when you gave your life to Jesus? I was so proud of you, I thought my heart would burst. You've grown in your faith over these past few years," her voice thickened, "and I couldn't love or be more proud of you. But if you're going to continue to follow Jesus, you're going to have to surrender these feelings and ask God to heal you. Pastor Jim can help you with that."

I couldn't breathe. I had to get out of the room. Away from her. I stood up fast, too fast, and my chair crashed to the floor. She jumped, splashing hot coffee over her arm.

"Ouch!" She turned the faucet on and shoved her arm under the stream of cold water.

"Mom, are you okay?" I asked, but she refused to answer or look at me. "Fine," I whispered.

"Of course it's fine. It's just a little burn." Her long brown hair hung over her face, but I didn't need to see her to know she was crying.

"I mean…fine, I'll go. I'll meet with Pastor Jim." I walked out of the kitchen, leaving her to tend her wounds. I had my own to think about.

Alone, in my bedroom, it surfaced. The feeling started in the back of my throat. Like an itch I couldn't scratch because I'd have to claw through skin and muscle and tendon and blood to reach it so it stayed there, throbbing and driving me mad.

I told him about everything that happened last summer. What's happening now. Except Mom didn't have a clue what was happening now.

If you're going to continue to follow Jesus, you're going to have to surrender these feelings and ask God to heal you. My throat constricted. I walked to the window. The glass felt cool against my flushed cheek. A cold front was moving in, bringing with it a change of seasons. I cracked the window and winced as the breeze bit into my skin. It rushed me. Pushed its way through the gap in the window until I stood there, gulping in the night air as I pictured my father, leaning against the tank, covered in Kevlar and smiling as the desert sand swirled around him. Had learning the truth about me finally wiped that smile from his face?

I dug my cell out of my pocket and texted Ian. No response. Desperate, I called another number, the one saved under SOS in my phone. The phone rang for what seemed like forever, and then I heard his voice.

"Hello? I'm here. Sorry! I couldn't find my phone!"

In my head, I said, *Hello, it's Jonathan. I could use your advice about something.* In reality, I stuttered, "Itsj-j-jonathan needtot-t-talktoyou," which trailed off into something even less comprehensible.

"Jonathan? Is that you? What's wrong?" The tension drained from my muscles. A true friend is someone who understands your stuttering sobs.

"I'm in trouble, Simon. I need your help."

"Take a deep breath and tell me what's going on."

An hour later, I hung up the phone, all cried out. Nothing had changed, and yet everything had changed because Simon, my former counselor at Spirit Lake Bible Camp and the truest friend of all, had promised to help me.

❖

Sketch leaned against my locker after school on Thursday.

"Hey, you mind?" She scooted over but not before she shot a dirty glance at me. "What's your issue now?" I twirled the combination lock until it clicked in my hands. I opened my locker and grabbed my backpack.

"I want you to ask Coach Thomas."

"Sketch, give it a break! I already know what he'd say." I slammed the door and turned to look at her. Just then Pete, Brandon, and Luke walked by us.

"Hey, Cooper, don't forget which bathroom to use," Pete said.

"See what I mean?" Sketch ranted as Pete turned away, laughing.

"I'm not disagreeing that a GSA would be great, but no teacher here is going to back us."

"Then we'll back ourselves." Sketch turned her attention to Pete. "Watch and learn, Padawan."

"I thought I was the Doctor?" I called after her as she walked toward Pete, but she wasn't listening to me anymore.

"Hey, Pete." She tapped him on the shoulder.

He turned around and sneered at her. "What do you want, fag hag?"

"Apologize. Now." Sketch took a step closer toward him. Pete grabbed her arm with one hand and looked toward Brandon and Luke as if to say *now this is going to be fun.*

I suppose that was the moment she'd been waiting for because he never saw it coming. Her knee shot up and nailed him right in the jewels. He crumpled to the ground, grabbed his nuts, and whimpered.

"You are a miserable skid mark in the toilet bowl of humanity! Lay one hand on either of us again and you'll need medical help to extract a banana from *your* ass. Got it?"

Pete's groan was technically open to interpretation, but lucky for him Sketch took it to mean he got it. She left him there, lying on the floor and grabbing his crotch in the middle of the hallway, and walked back to me.

"I sort of love you," I told her, not one word of it a lie.

"Yeah, yeah. I get that a lot." She looped her arm through mine and pulled me toward the front door. "Too bad you're taken. So, what's your plan?"

"My plan?" I blinked. "I don't think Pete can take any more. As it is, he's going to be spending the night with a bag of frozen peas wedged inside his underwear."

"Gross!" Sketch frowned, but I didn't buy it. Just the thought of Pete in misery had made her all twitchy in her fishnet nylons and combat boots, like she wanted nothing more than one last stomp on his face. "You could have spared me that visual. No, that little turd is small potatoes. I'm talking about your real problem." She slow-walked, her hips swaying side to side, tweeting one-handed on her cell phone that Pete Mitchell needed a bag of frozen peas ASAP while excavating her purse with her other hand until she triumphantly retrieved a tube of lipstick. She puckered her lips and smeared another layer of black gloss, and I swear to God all I could see was Dad applying camouflage paint before he went into battle. "You've got your one-on-one with Pastor Jim today, right? You need to have a war plan. Have your shields up before he throws Leviticus at you or something."

"Wait, I'm confused. Now you're channeling James T. Kirk?" I teased her.

Sketch laughed. "All the best teachings about life can be found in science fiction."

We reached the front door, and I held it open for her.

"You're hopeless. You know that, right?" I'd meant it to be just another jab in the back-and-forth that defined our friendship, but the look on her face told me I'd failed.

"No, I'm not and neither are you and neither is the GSA." She stared into my eyes, then darted up and kissed me, no doubt leaving a streak of black across my cheek. No, not that kind of a kiss. It wasn't like that. It was more like Sketch signing her name on one of her many canvases.

"Remember, shields up!" Her voice followed me as I walked down the school steps.

❖

"You didn't need to take off work to come with me." Mom and I were waiting in the church office. She lifted her head from her Bible to glance at me, then resumed reading without saying a word. "You thought I wouldn't show, didn't you?"

She closed her Bible. "Actually, Jonathan, I took the day off because I had a doctor's appointment this morning."

"Oh." I smiled at Mrs. Fields, the church secretary, and walked over to the window. Outside, the trees looked like they were under fire, their branches flaming red and whipping in the wind.

"Jonathan, I'm worried about you. You never have Pete or any of your other friends over anymore. You only hang out with that sketchy girl."

"Believe me, I see plenty of Pete. And it's Sketch, Mom. Her name is Sketch."

"What kind of a name is *Sketch?*"

I ignored the question since it wasn't worth answering.

"Fine. Her name is Sketch," Mom said. "Jonathan, I wish you'd look at me. I'm just trying to help you."

I pulled my eyes away from the window and stared at her. "By forcing me to talk about this with Pastor Jim? I don't think so."

"He's known you since you were a baby. He baptized and confirmed you. I can't think of a better person for you to talk with about…this problem." Mom lowered her voice and looked around.

I snorted. "How are we supposed to fix *this problem* if you can't even say the word?"

Mom turned her attention back to something she understood, her Bible. "Pastor Jim will help you get over this and be yourself again."

"Your assumption is erroneous." I smiled slowly, enjoying the look of confusion that spread across her face.

"My assumption is what?" Her voice rose. She shot a glance at Mrs. Fields and forced herself to whisper. "What are you talking about?"

"It means I am being myself."

"Don't say that!" Her voice bordered on a wail. Evidently, we were beyond caring about impressing Mrs. Fields.

"Why not, Mom? It's the truth."

The door opened and Pastor Jim emerged. "Linda and Jonathan! I'm sorry I kept you waiting. Why don't we step into my office and talk?"

Mom stood and smoothed her skirt. She walked over to shake Pastor Jim's hand. Armed with her Bible and a perfectly lipsticked smile that did not camouflage her desperation, she waited for me to join her.

There was no alternative. No choice. No way out.

"Shields up, my ass," I mumbled to Sketch, who wasn't there to fight this battle for me. "I'd rather have Scotty beam me the hell out of here!"

"What was that, Jonathan?" Pastor Jim looked at me.

"Nothing. It was nothing." I followed them through the opened door.

Pastor Jim's office was just like him. Comfortably disorganized. Books were piled on the floor. His desk was a mess, but the clutter only told half the story. Pictures filled his walls and covered the credenza. Pastor Jim in the Boundary Waters with a boatload of kids, including me. Pastor Jim visiting a sick kid in a hospital. Pastor Jim perched on a roof, hammer in hand. That was the summer we'd built a house in Mexico for Habitat for Humanity.

"Thank you for seeing us. I can't tell you what a relief it is!" Mom moved a pile of newspapers and sank into a chair in front of Pastor Jim's desk. I sat in the chair next to her.

He reached across the desk and patted Mom's arm. "Linda, we are one family in Christ. I know you are facing a struggle, but I also want you to remember that nothing is beyond God's ability to heal."

"Amen." She nodded and brushed a tear away from her eye.

"I'm glad you came today, but if it's all right with you, I'd like to speak with Jonathan alone."

A chill prickled my skin.

"Of course. I feel so much better already. I'll wait in the

office." Mom stood to leave. She smiled as she faced me, but her eyes said something different. *You will cooperate!*

"So, Jonathan," Pastor Jim said once my mother left his office. "I hear you had quite the summer. Care to tell me about it?"

Not particularly. "I met someone. His name is Ian. We... uh...we...uh..."

"Okay, I get it." Pastor Jim ended my misery. "You don't have to tell me anything about that right now. What's important is that you know what happened was not your fault. It doesn't make you a bad person."

I know that! I wanted to scream. *But do you?*

"You're in the grips of temptation, Jonathan, but your true identity comes from God. He has given you this male body, and He intends you to be a strong man of God and that, my friend, is the truth that can set you free. Do you want to be set free, Jonathan?"

I froze, unable to respond. Free of the rumors? Free of Pete's abuse? Free of the guilt I felt for hurting my parents? Free of loving Ian? Free of feeling real in my skin? Free of believing that God could love me as I am?

Pastor Jim pulled a brochure out of a drawer and slid it across to me. "I know of a program that counsels individuals who want to leave the gay lifestyle. I think they could help you, Jonathan."

"But I don't want to—"

"Don't want to what? Obey God's word?"

"I don't know. That's not what I meant." My head spun. I gripped the arms of the chair and tried to find up and down again.

Pastor Jim stood and walked around his desk. He stood beside me and laid his hand on my back. "Father God, please be with Jonathan as he walks through this dark valley of confusion. Help him to remember who You created him to be, and please help me to guide him along that journey."

❖

Emergency! Call me! I texted Ian as I left Mom in the living room, her nose buried in the brochure for Deliverance Clinic, and walked up the stairs to my bedroom. I closed the door just as he called.

His voice was lotion on a sunburn. "Hey, what's up?"

I swallowed and tried to find the words. "Mom made me go see Pastor Jim. He gave us a brochure for a counselor who specializes in reparative therapy."

Silence. Followed by more silence.

"Ian, you there?"

"Listen up. Here's what we're going to do."

Ian went on to outline a plan that involved vandalizing Deliverance Clinic and then running away to some state in the South. When I asked him *why the South,* he replied that we might have to sleep under bridges until we could get an apartment.

"You could get a job at a photography store and I could write for the newspapers. Maybe a column. I think I'd like that. And we could get a studio apartment. We don't need much room."

The more he talked, the faster and higher his voice got. In the background, I could hear him opening and closing drawers. It was up to me to throw a big ol' bucket of reality on the situation.

"What are you doing?" I asked him.

"Packing! Aren't you?"

"Ian, can we be real for a second?"

"What do you mean *be real*?"

"I mean, we're sixteen."

"What we are is screwed. What does being sixteen have to do with anything?"

"What do you mean? *We're* screwed? Is something wrong?" I asked, but he ignored the question.

"Don't bother about me. You need to start packing."

I sighed. "You're talking crazy. We'd maybe get to Iowa and then our money would run out. Do you know how cold winters are in Iowa?"

Silence. Then, "You don't want to go away with me?"

"It's not that. It's—" I didn't know how to put in words what it was.

"No, I get it. You'd rather bitch to me about hitting a road bump in your otherwise perfect life than hitting the road and making a new life with me."

I tried to explain how my life was anything but perfect, but he hung up on me. Just what I needed. On top of the fact that Mom was seriously considering sending me to sexual reparative therapy, Ian was pissed I wouldn't run away with him. The whole world had gone crazy.

I fell into a fitful sleep and dreamt of standing with Ian outside Deliverance Clinic. It was huge and imposing in my imagination with black windows and stark white concrete brick walls.

Do it, Ian said. I lifted my arm and pushed my finger down on the nozzle. The steady spray of red paint sputtered mid capital R and died. I took a step back and examined the splotch of paint.

ABEN'T isn't a word. Ian stated the obvious.

Thanks. I didn't know that. I gave the can a violent shake. A ball pinged inside the metal can, stirring things up.

Ian glanced around the deserted street before walking

over to the window on the side of the wall. I knew what he was thinking. I was thinking the same thing.

I took off my jacket and wrapped it around my fist. It was hard to restrain myself. The temptation to smash the window to smithereens was overwhelming, but that would have been counterproductive. The faint tinkling of glass as it hit the concrete was an insult.

I waited, ready to run at the first blast of an alarm. Nothing. I looked around for Ian, but he'd disappeared around the building to keep a lookout.

I reached through the broken window and opened the door. It was dark inside the clinic. I pressed the button on my flashlight, but nothing happened.

"Eveready, my ass." The flashlight smashed into the whiteboard in what appeared to be a conference room and bounced off the words I recognized from the brochure.

If your hand or foot causes you to stumble, cut it off, and cast it from you. It is better for you to enter into life maimed or crippled, rather than having two hands or two feet to be cast into the eternal fire. If your eye causes you to stumble, pluck it out, and cast it from you. It is better for you to enter into life with one eye, rather than having two eyes to be cast into the fire of hell.—Matthew 18: 8–9

I grabbed the spray cleaner for the whiteboard and a roll of paper towels and crawled back out the window. It took a bit of scrubbing, but eventually, the R no longer looked like a B… much. I dropped the paper towels on the ground and stepped toward the clinic wall again.

Another shake of the can. Ping ping.

B…

My shoulder ached as I guided the crimson stream.

R…*O*…

"Tell them," Ian said. "Tell everyone!"

K...E...N!

I stepped back to examine my work. Long ribbons of red snaked down the wall from the foot-high letters. Ian slid his body next to mine and we stood there, shoulder to shoulder.

YOU CAN'T FIX US BECAUSE WE AREN'T BROKEN!

My shoulders unknotted as I listened to Ian read it aloud. The nearly empty can of spray paint slipped from my hand and clattered to the ground.

He reached for me, his thin arms wrapping around me until the shaking stopped. "Now let's head south," he said. "I'm thinking Orlando. We could get jobs working at Walt Disney World."

I woke up, covered in sweat, with thoughts of Mickey Mouse and Cinderella's castle swirling through my mind.

CHAPTER FIFTEEN

I didn't run away. I got up the next morning and had breakfast with my mother, who prayed *Lord, give us the courage to confront our sinful natures* before she sliced bananas into my bowl of Rice Krispies, and I went to school.

"How did it go?" Sketch added flecks of blue-white to the background of her *Dying Dove* canvas. She dug through her supplies, pulled out a scraggly brush, and dipped it in water. She leaned in toward her canvas and touched the dried red paint, turning it instantly into a red blob. "Goddammit!" She flung the brush against the wall and stuck a rag on the blob. "I need new art supplies!"

I ignored her tirade. "It sucked. He gave my mother a brochure for Deliverance Clinic."

"What? The place that tries to fix gay people?"

"Yeah, but don't worry. I'm not going."

She turned from her canvas and cocked an eyebrow at me. "Really? And how are you going to manage that?"

"Simple, I called in reinforcements."

"Reinforcements? What do you mean?"

"I mean it's my turn to take you someplace."

"Where?"

The moment deserved to be savored. "My TARDIS, my

rules. Just meet me in the parking lot after school." I turned my attention to the photo shoot I had been arranging. An idea I'd gotten from Ms. Owens and her gourds. Two mannequins "borrowed" from home ec's sewing class. Some assembly required. Two crowns "found" in the theater prop room. Maybe yelling wasn't the only way to earn Robert Mapplethorpe's approval.

"Interesting, Jonathan! Are you shooting this in black and white?" Ms. Owens helped me attach the arms.

"Thanks, and yeah. Black and white." I positioned the mannequin in what I hoped resembled a dancing stance and locked it in place.

"What's your inspiration?" Ms. Owens asked. Sketch snorted in the background and continued her quest to blend blood and snow.

"Love, Ms. Owens. Just a little thing called love." I tried to balance a crown on the mannequin's head, but it slipped and plunged toward the floor. I grabbed it midair.

Eventually, I got them perfect. Two men dancing. Both wearing crowns with one resting his head on the other's shoulder exactly like the Robert Mapplethorpe photograph. I tried to replicate the basics of it, but everything—every speed setting, every angle, every aperture size—made me want to smash my camera against the wall.

"Excuse me, Sketch. Could you move? Just a little bit to the left?" I carried a light box over to where she had her canvas set up. It was the perfect spot, I was certain.

"Seriously, Jonathan? Again?" She grabbed her easel and moved, though not without shooting a dirty look at me.

"Sorry! I'm not getting this lighting right." I set up the light box and angled it underneath the mannequins. Maybe all it needed was a spot of uplighting?

I shot a few pictures, skipping around the room to get different angles.

"Oh, for God's sake!" Sketch yelled when I bumped into her, sending her palette flying to the floor. "They're bloody mannequins! A bunch of plastic arms and legs. Fake faces. What do you expect? That they're going to just come to life and look like the Mapplethorpe?"

It was a good thing Ms. Owens was across the room, studying an unfortunate painting of distinctly non-gourd-like looking gourds. Only Mason, Sketch, and I knew that I was trying (and failing) to reproduce *Two Men Dancing*.

"She has a point." Mason appeared beside me as I scowled into my viewfinder.

"Which is?" Occasionally, Mason had flashes of genius. There was no disputing the fact.

"Mapplethorpe photographed in black and white, right?"

"Right."

"Black-and-white is a medium of exaggeration. Whatever is real becomes more real."

I thought of all the reasons I loved black-and-white photography. Truth laid bare inside the shades of gray. As usual, Mason was correct.

"Your point?"

"Whatever is fake is more fake. It's not your camera or your setting or your speed or your light or your angle. It's your medium. You need a splash of color." He walked away, the corner of his mouth twitching. "Let me know if you need help in that department. It's a specialty of mine."

Of course I hadn't thought to bring clothes for the mannequins to wear, a fact that sent Mason into a dervish of activity, plundering one student's hat, Sketch's scarf, another student's cardigan, even Ms. Owen's purse, which he deemed large enough to be considered a "man bag" while I switched to the full color setting on my Nikon. To be fair, Mason also sacrificed his own shirt for the project and stood there shirtless after the shoot, admiring the results while I admired his abs.

❖

The rain started halfway through another soccer practice from hell where I spent most of it on the bench, wishing umbrellas were standard soccer equipment. By the end, it was freezing rain, but with just one week until homecoming, Coach Thomas wasn't about to cancel practice early. I found Sketch and Mason shivering by my dad's beat-up Honda.

"Let's go!"

"You're not seriously planning on taking your dad's car out in this mess?" Mason looked at the sheets of icy rain that fell from the sky.

"I most certainly am!" I unlocked my car. "There's someone you both have to meet!"

"I'm not sure this is a good idea."

"Quit being such a wuss, Mason." Sketch called shotgun, and Mason crawled into the backseat of the car.

To Sketch and Mason's credit, it took one second to convince them that the perfectly reasonable thing to do was to skate over Highway 35W to I-94 where only about a million or so cars would be reenacting a bumper car scene right out of Valleyfair Amusement Park simply because I told them they would regret it for the rest of their lives if they didn't go. It's a quality all friends should have but, sadly, few do. Neither of them once uttered the words *but what if you wreck your dad's car,* and for that, I loved them more than ever.

For the record, speeding on slick roads in the late fall in Minneapolis is a bad idea. The red octagon sign with the word STOP at the corner of Lake and Lyndale was coated with ice, but yeah, I saw it. If we ever covered the topic *how not to run over a stop sign in an ice storm* in driver's ed, I didn't remember anything. I slammed my foot on the brake. The car and I had a moment of disagreement, which resolved quickly and not in my favor. The car's back end spun in a frantic circle.

"No, no, no, NO!" I shouted, but not as loudly as Mason, whose shriek from the backseat almost shattered my windshield. I flung my arm across Sketch's chest when the car's wheels hit a patch of ice and slid to the left, missing the sign by inches. We sat in silence, panting like chain smokers in the cold air.

"You can stop groping me now," Sketch said, her giggle half panic and half relief.

"Sorry," I mumbled, removing my hand from her breast.

"That's okay. For a minute there I almost understood what Ian sees in you." Her cheeks flushed red. Not from the cold, if I had to guess.

I spotted the store down the street. A large willow tree painting filled the entire front window. Its curlicues were every hue of the rainbow: lime, celadon, turquoise, fuchsia. I maneuvered the car into an open spot in front of it and parked. "We're here."

"*Young at Art,*" Sketch read from the sign above the door. "You almost killed a stop sign, not to mention the three of us, for art supplies? Because I don't need new brushes that badly."

"I don't need anything that badly," Mason grumbled, which earned another *quit being such a wuss* from Sketch.

A blast of freezing rain pelted the windshield. "There's someone you both have to meet. He's sort of like Professor X, only cooler."

"No one is cooler than Professor X." Sketch shivered and reached for her door handle.

Young at Art's front door opened to the cheerful sound of a bell tinkling, and we stepped inside.

"Wow, wow, wow, wow!" Sketch fixated on the lake scene that covered the entire wall to our left. Composed of thousands of bits of broken glass, it rippled sapphire and aqua.

"Check this out!" Mason swiveled to look at the mural that covered the wall to our right. A lush forest of birch and fir trees and a winding pathway stretched before us. Just the way I remembered it. My breath caught in my throat. Simon had brought the mural to life by adding bushes in planter boxes and a cobblestone path that sprouted out of the painting and wove through the knotty pine floor throughout the entire front room. I looked up, knowing exactly what I would see. An indigo night sky with a thousand twinkling lights. He had captured it all.

"Okay, he might be as cool as Professor X." Sketch walked down the cobblestone path, her eyes darting over Simon's paintings that hung on the exposed brick wall. "Who is this guy and how do you know him, and, most importantly, why haven't you brought us here before?"

From the back room, I heard a deep baritone chuckle and looked toward the open doorway. His footrest wheeled into view first. Then his knees, and finally, Simon himself. I met him halfway and knelt to hug him.

"Oh man, I have missed you!" I whispered into his flannel shirt and inhaled the scent of cedar, sage, and paint thinner.

"Let me look at you!" Simon pulled away and studied my eyes, my face, my hair that had grown even shaggier in the three months since I'd seen him. "It's good to see you, Jonathan, and you've brought guests!"

Sketch's eyes darted from Simon's wheelchair to the painted ceiling to the twelve-foot-tall mural to his wheelchair again.

I laughed as her eyebrows disappeared behind her black jagged bangs. "Simon, this is my friend Sketch."

For a moment, I wondered what he would think of the fishnet nylons, combat boots, and jet-black lipstick, and then I remembered. This was Simon.

He wheeled toward her, his gaze never leaving her eyes. "It's so nice to meet another artist!" He held out his hand and smiled.

Sketch took two steps forward, shook his hand, and sank onto one of the wooden benches that were scattered throughout the room. "I love your store. It's…" For the first time since I'd known her, Sketch was speechless.

"Thank you. It was a collaborative effort that involved a hydraulic lift, a beautiful woman, the world's biggest dog, and yours truly." Simon smiled and looked at Mason. "And you are?"

"Mason. Sort of an artist too, but not like Sketch. I'm a fashion designer."

"There is no such thing as a *sort of artist,*" Simon said. "If you need to create, then you are an artist. Welcome to Young at Art."

"This place is amazing, Simon. Where are Dawn and Bear?" I asked, my eyes wandering around the store for my second-favorite camp counselor, an Ojibwe woman who believed I was on a spirit quest, and her ginormous dog.

"Bear has been bouncing off the walls all morning, so Dawn took him for a walk. I should warn you, Jonathan, he's grown since you saw him last." The door tinkled behind us, and we turned just in time to see a white blur bound through the doorway immediately followed by a woman with long dark hair and copper skin. The dog crouched down for a moment and then shook like an earthquake, the ripples starting at his shoulders and reverberating through his back and full tail. His long white fur swung toward us, flinging sheets of freezing water.

"Oh man, Bear!" I shouted. He froze at the sound of my voice, his ears twitching.

"No, *Makwa! Namadabin!*" Dawn tightened her grip on the leash too late. It slipped through her fingers as Bear charged me. I had just enough time to realize that Bear had stopped listening to Ojibwe before he launched himself at me, sending me to the ground where he crawled on me and commenced full-body licking. Mason and Sketch darted forward and begin wrestling the one-hundred-twenty-pound dog with little success while Simon sat in his chair, his rich chortle echoing through the room.

"I liked this more when he did it to Ian." The thought flitted through my mind and out my mouth, which was a big mistake. "Getimoffrme!" I shouted, despite the fact that a Great Pyrenees was conducting a thorough examination of my tonsils with his tongue. "P-puhleese!"

Sketch grabbed his tail while Dawn clamped her arms around Bear's chest, and together, they wrestled him off me before he could commence full-body licking. "We start obedience classes next week," Dawn offered as an apology.

"Which I keep telling her is a waste of good money," Simon said. Bear gave up and rolled onto his back as if he'd somehow earned a belly rub.

"I see things haven't changed a bit." I stroked his stomach.

But of course they had, which was the reason I had brought Mason and Sketch to Young at Art. We moved into the classroom in the back of the studio where Sketch drooled over Simon's never-ending art supplies while Mason and I checked out the kiln and pottery wheel. Dawn served us tea out of pottery mugs at a worktable, and I told Simon and Dawn everything. About the text that had been sent to everyone at school and Pete grinding my face into a urinal cake and my mother telling my father and Pastor Jim and his brochure for Deliverance Clinic. When I got to the part where we wanted to start a GSA, but no teacher at East Bay would be our advisor, Simon interrupted, "I thought GSA clubs were student led."

"They usually are," Mason said. "But private schools can make whatever rules they want."

"And one of the ways they keep GSA clubs out is to require an advisor when they know full well no one on the faculty would dare accept the position. Smart, huh?" Sketch glared.

"You're generous. I would have chosen a different word." Simon shook his head.

"But the school handbook doesn't say *faculty* advisor. It just says *advisor*." I waited, knowing Simon.

He looked at Dawn.

"You said you felt led to this place. Maybe this is the reason." She rested her hand on his.

"Just so we're clear, even with an advisor, the board of trustees could still try to prevent this," Simon pointed out.

"I know just the way to deal with those idiots." Sketch dug a business card out of her purse and handed it to him. He read it and raised an eyebrow.

"Even if we pull this off, have you thought about what life will be like for the three of you at school?"

"We're already living it," I said.

"All right then." Simon drove the chill away that had settled in my bones. "Who do I call?"

CHAPTER SIXTEEN

Rev. Dimmesdale knocks up Hester Prynne and then lets her face all those pricks by herself? That's your idea of a hero?" Pete shook his head in disgust the next morning in American lit.

"What should he have done? Turn himself in to be hanged?" Mason argued.

"At least he would have died a real man." Pete glanced at me.

Mason's face flushed red. "And you know all about what it means to be a real man, do you?"

"More than you do, that's for damn sure!"

Mr. Gilchrist stood up from behind his desk and raised his hands. "Gentlemen, let's take a step back for a moment, why don't we? While I'm delighted that you are moved to such intensity by *The Scarlet Letter,* I'm not sure—"

With all the shouting going on, no one, not even Mr. Gilchrist, had noticed the door opening or the girl who held out the slip of paper. "Excuse me, I have a note from the office. Sorry to bother you."

"No bother. Bit of a relief, actually." Mr. Gilchrist crossed the room and read the note. "It seems this discussion will need to be continued later. Mason and Jonathan, you're both wanted in Principal Hardin's office."

I looked at Mason; he looked at me. *Simon.* I mouthed the word and he nodded. We gathered our stuff as the class oohed and aahed, no doubt imagining all sorts of impending punishments for nonexistent infractions.

We walked into Principal Hardin's office and found Sketch, sitting in the farthest chair with a folder on her lap, waiting for us. Behind the dark cherry desk, Principal Hardin scowled. My stomach twisted as I sat beside Sketch. Mason slumped into the seat next to me.

"Would one of you care to tell me who"—Principal Hardin glanced down at a piece of paper with scribbling on his desk—"Simon Fletcher is?"

I spoke first. "He was my camp counselor."

"He's an artist," Mason continued.

And Sketch brought it home. "He's the advisor of our Gay-Straight Alliance."

Principal Hardin's face flushed. "But this Simon Fletcher is not a faculty member!"

Sketch opened the folder and slid a piece of paper across his desk. "I believe you'll see that the East Bay Christian Academy school manual clearly states that an advisor is only required to be a qualified adult. It does not state that an advisor must be a teacher at this school. Simon Fletcher not only holds his bachelor's degree in art and theology, he has been a counselor at Spirit Lake Bible Camp for the past four years. He is the owner of Young at Art, a studio, where he teaches art to children."

Principal Hardin scoured the sheet of paper, photocopied from his own school manual, his face mottling more by the second.

"Young lady, I have no doubt that Simon Fletcher is fully

qualified to be an advisor in this school, but that is simply not the only issue at hand today. May I remind you that you are a student at East Bay *Christian* Academy?"

Sketch leaned forward and stared into Principal Hardin's eyes. I almost felt sorry for him. Almost, but not quite.

"Sure, but I'd like to remind you of something as well. I may be a student at this school, but I am also Liam and Catherine Mallory's daughter." She opened her folder again, took out two business cards, and slid them across the desk to Principal Hardin. "Maybe you've heard of the law offices of Mallory & Mallory? It's one of the top law firms in the nation, specializing in criminal and civil law. In other words, they kick ass in the courtroom."

If the word *ass* made Principal Hardin scowl, the word *courtroom* made him shudder.

Sketch continued, "My parents asked me to inform you that they are more than happy to discuss objections to a peaceful club dedicated to creating a safe school for all students, gay or straight, with you or any member of the board of trustees. Their number is on their card."

"You GO, girl!" Mason slapped his hand on Principal Hardin's desk, which was just so Mason I couldn't help but laugh.

Hardin raised his hand and silenced us. Well, almost. Mason tried to look serious, but a random giggle or two escaped nonetheless. "It seems, Frances, that you have thought this through." Principal Hardin stared at the business cards. "I wonder though if you may have forgotten something. As you know, all co-curricular clubs meet after school between the hours of three and five p.m."

My stomach clenched.

"Are you quite certain you will have the requisite three students to meet during that time frame?"

Sketch and Mason looked at me.

"Yes, sir." I swallowed. "We have the necessary three students." I fought the urge to storm out of his office and smash the glass display case, the one with the soccer trophies I'd helped put there.

"Jonathan, you don't have to do this." Mason read my face. "No, Sketch. We can't ask him to do this." He silenced her before she could object.

"It's done, Mason." I stood and walked out the door. It didn't matter to me whether I had Principal Hardin's permission to leave. I knew what I had to do, and there was no point in putting it off.

I found Coach Thomas supervising study hall in his classroom. The conversation was short and sweet. In fact, when I told him I was quitting so I could start a Gay-Straight Alliance, he didn't say one word.

Ian, however, had plenty to say when I told him what happened.

The current temperature in Orlando is a balmy 83 degrees, he texted me. *It's 78 and sunny in San Francisco.*

CHAPTER SEVENTEEN

"Ian's your what?" Grace asks again.

"He's my boyfriend." I watch her face for it, *the look,* but it never appears.

"Tell me about him." She rocks back and forth in her chair as if she has eternity to listen to me talk about Ian.

"He's short." I don't know why that is the first thing that comes out of my mouth, but it is. I rush to add more. "And he's got red hair and loads of freckles and green eyes with little flecks of gold."

Grace nods. "That's what he looks like. I'd like to hear about the things that matter."

"Oh. Let's see. He's a writer. He knows more words than Mr. Gilchrist. Maybe even more than Nathaniel Hawthorne." I feel it, the swell of pride that rises in me whenever I think of Ian and his writing.

"I am familiar with Mr. Hawthorne, but you'll have to help me with Mr. Gilchrist."

"He's my American lit teacher."

"I see. Continue, please."

"He also directs the plays at school."

"I meant continue with more about Ian. Where did you meet him?"

I almost hear it, the faint lulling sound of waves washing against the shore. The love song of the cricket. The incessant hum of the mosquitoes. The sound of laughter and the splash of cannonballs off the dock. "At Spirit Lake Bible Camp," I tell her. "I met him last summer."

"You fell in love with a boy? At a Bible camp?"

I am sure the look will appear then, but as Grace's forehead creases, I realize that the wrinkles around her eyes have nothing to do with disapproval.

"I'm sure that was scary for you."

I don't know what to say. I'd like to tell her that she's right, but she's got the tense wrong. Not *was*. *Is* scary.

"What was it about Ian that drew you to him?"

That question stumps me. I stutter, reaching for words that should come more easily. "He's strong. The strongest person on the planet. He'll fight anyone. Anytime. It doesn't matter if they're bigger or meaner or if there are three or thirty of them."

"I can see why you loved him."

"No. You keep getting the tenses wrong." My throat constricts as if someone were holding a cold blade against it to keep the words in, but I push past the pressure. "I *love* him."

She pats my hand. "Of course you do. You look exhausted, Jonathan. Why don't you get some rest?"

The darkness sneaks up on me, and, before I know it, I am drifting away.

CHAPTER EIGHTEEN

Absolutely *not*! I forbid it!" Mom walked toward me, waving a roller brush saturated with paint. "Sounds of Nature," an odious shade of green, obviously not chosen for the name. Who could possibly think that a bathroom needed *more* sounds of nature?

"It's done," I said for the second time that day. "Whether you forbid it or not."

"I don't understand! What's happening to you?" She stood in the hallway between the bathroom and the living room, her body swaying as if she'd been punched.

I took a step closer to her. "Nothing's happening to me, Mom. Why can't you see this is just who I am?"

She held the brush out to stop me. "Because this is *not* who you are, Jonathan. Quitting soccer to start a Gay-Straight..."

"Alliance."

She shook her head. "No, you're confused. The people at Deliverance Clinic will sort this out." She put the brush in the tray and started pushing buttons on her cell.

"Go ahead! Make an appointment! You can't make me go to it!" I headed for the front door.

"Jonathan, you come back here. We are not done—*Hello. My name is Linda Cooper, and I was wondering if you might have any openings this week...*"

I slammed the door behind me, not because I needed to make my point, but because it felt damn good. The blast of cold air on my face did nothing to cool me down as I stood on the front steps, my cell in my shaking hands.

She's making an appointment, I texted Ian. *What am I going to do?* My breath came in short, jagged bursts.

You declined my suggestion, he replied.

Ian, get real! I texted. *They'd find us!*

Good luck at your appointment then. Tell me how it goes. The smartass.

I thought about the appointment Mom had certainly made for me at Deliverance Clinic. It hit me then—the fact that Simon, though he could solve the advisor issue for the GSA at school—was powerless to stop her from hauling my ass into that clinic. And Ian? His only solution was to run away, which was no solution at all.

The blood in my temples throbbed, building into a crescendo of sound that threatened to burst my skull.

"What the hell?" The sound was not inside my head. I glared at the car parked across the street from my house. At the driver who sat behind the steering wheel, his breath fogging up his window. "Enough, already!" I shouted. "Whoever you're waiting for knows you're here!"

The window lowered and a gloved hand emerged, waving at me. "Hey! Over here!"

I peered at the person in the car. Blond. Stylish sunglasses. Camel-colored scarf wrapped around the raised collar of a black peacoat. I shoved my cell in my pocket and sprinted to the car. I yanked on the handle. Nothing.

"Sorry!" Mason leaned over the passenger seat and opened the door.

It was all the invitation I needed as I sank into the bucket seat. We rode without speaking for a while, his jacked-up sound system thumping out a bass beat that rattled my teeth. Even though the metallic lenses of his sunglasses made it impossible to know for sure, I felt him glance at me every now and then. It weirded me out a bit, so I spent the car ride looking at anything but Mason. The dust-free dashboard. The shining steering wheel that he held at precisely ten and two o'clock. The floor mats that were cleaner than the carpet in my house.

"Where are we going?" I found my voice when he exited onto Highway 494 East.

"That depends on you." He took his sunglasses off and looked at me, his dark eyes steamy and warm. "Any requests?"

"Paris."

"Tempting, but this is a Subaru, not a submersible. Second choice?"

"You tricked out a Subaru?" I smirked.

"Home then?"

"Sorry. It's a snazzy car. Just grand. How about Orlando? I hear it's eighty-three degrees there. San Francisco's nice too. Do you mind if we make a short detour to Wisconsin first?"

Mason slid a sideways glance at me. His eyes asked the question, *how close to Nutsville are you?* "I take it you want to escape the suburbs?"

"God, yes."

"You got it." He hit the CD button, and the music changed. A man's voice with equal parts yearning and knowing swirled around me.

I closed my eyes, trusting the music and Mason to take me where I needed to go.

I kept my eyes shut even after the CD ended. Even after the car slowed and then stopped. Even after Mason whispered, "Jonathan, we're here."

When I did open my eyes, I saw that he'd brought me to a café-bar called the Crisis Pointe. Dude had a seriously whacked sense of humor. Inside, it was dark and smelled of stale cigar smoke and skunk, which Mason assured me meant someone had spilled Heineken beer. We chose a booth toward the back of the café where we had to squint at each other.

"We'll have two pints of dark ale," Mason told the waitress. "Your finest, please."

She laughed at him in the face and he regained some dignity by ordering two espressos. The waitress walked off without an answer, and when she returned, she brought us two coffees, pitch-black and bitter, and we drank them in the dark.

"Thanks," I said when the caffeine kicked in.

"No prob. I was worried about you."

"So you sat outside my house, waiting, in case I showed up looking like I wanted to run away?"

"No." The corners around Mason's dark ale, make that espresso-colored, eyes crinkled. "I was just about to go knock on your door when you showed up on the front step looking like you wanted to run away."

"Good timing." I shoveled a third teaspoon of sugar into the coffee and then a fourth. By the sixth, the stuff was finally drinkable.

He moved his hand close to the middle of the table, but not quite over it.

"So, next week is homecoming."

"And I bailed on my team right before the big game against Sacred Heart. Thanks for rubbing it in."

Mason shook his head. "That's not what I meant."

I raised the cup of sludge to my lips. I even drank it. It bought me a few seconds. "Then what?"

"I was, ah, wondering if you were planning on going to the homecoming dance."

Was he? No, of course not. I mean, he couldn't be. I put the coffee cup on the table and blurted out the first thing that felt normal. Safe. "Hell no! I'm not facing those guys after the game by myself."

"That settles it, then." Mason signaled for the bill. "You won't be by yourself."

My cell beeped inside my pocket. For once, I ignored it. If Ian wanted to apologize for calling my life perfect and hanging up on me, he'd damn well have to do better than texting me.

"I'm not?" I asked, confused.

"Definitely not." Mason gave the waitress a ten. "Keep the change," he told her. If she was grateful for the tip, she didn't show it.

I spent the ride home from the Crisis Pointe with my pulse tripping erratically due to the caffeine rush and thoughts of *holy shit I have to face my mother.* I steeled myself for whatever awaited me at home. Hysterical Mom. Silent Mom. Maybe even the staff of Deliverance Clinic ready to cart me off for admittance. I was prepared for anything. Anything, that is, except the sight of Dawn perched on the couch in the living room with Butler sprawled across her lap and purring louder than a John Deere tractor. It was Mom, across the room in Dad's recliner, who looked ready to scratch and hiss.

"Um, hello." I stood in the doorway, trying to decipher the scene in front of me.

"You didn't tell me we would be having a guest." Mom spoke in her hybrid voice. The one that was a cross between polite and pissed.

Dawn filled the awkward gap of my silence. "Oh, I'm afraid that's my fault, Mrs. Cooper. Jonathan didn't know I was coming over. It was a spur-of-the-moment idea that came to me in my prayers this morning. Please forgive me for not calling ahead." Dawn smiled. Mom appeared to relax a bit. Probably because Dawn had said the word *prayer*. I sank onto the couch next to Dawn, drawn to her the way a hypothermia victim huddles around an open fire.

"Please, call me Linda. No need to apologize. Any friend of Jon's is welcome here. How do you know my son again?"

"From Spirit Lake Bible camp. I help out with the nature classes when I'm not working for the DNR. At least, I used to."

"Oh, Dawn! Of course. Jonathan has spoken of you often." My mother remembered her manners. "Are you thirsty? Would you like something to eat?"

"That would be lovely," Dawn said, and my mother walked into the kitchen.

"What's going on?" I asked in the few minutes it would take Mom to dig through the cupboards.

"It sounded like you needed backup on both the school and the home front from what you said the other day at Young at Art," Dawn said, elusive as ever. "Simon can help you with the GSA, but I might be able to help you here."

"No offense, Dawn, but how can you help with my mom?"

"It's a woman thing," she said, to which I did not feel qualified to respond, even if there had been time.

"I hope you like lemon bars." Mom returned to the living

room and set a tray that contained a plate of bars and three glasses of iced tea on the coffee table.

"Delicious!" Dawn picked up a glass of tea. Though lemon bars were my favorite, my stomach churned as I looked at them. Dawn wasn't actually going to try to talk to Mom about me being gay, was she? My shoulders ached as I imagined repainting all the rooms in the house again.

"Would you mind if I said a blessing?" Dawn asked, and my mother smiled. "Dear Jesus, we thank You for living amongst us and for teaching us that our true purpose is to be a vehicle of Your love. Thank You for reminding us that everyone, especially those scorned by society, is cherished by our Father. Amen."

I opened my eyes and gently leaned into Dawn.

The lemon bar in Mom's hand trembled. Sprinkles of powdered sugar fell onto her pants. "That was lovely." Mom's voice broke slightly. Not quite a puberty moment, but close. "Now, what was it you wanted to talk to us about?"

Dawn took a sip of her tea and set it on the tray. A bead of condensation slid down the side of the glass.

"Jonathan probably mentioned that Simon and I moved to Minneapolis." Dawn paused when my mother looked perplexed. It was just one in the dozens of topics categorized under *things I haven't told my mother.* Dawn continued. "Anyway, we've joined One Heart, a progressive, non-denominational church in Minneapolis with an affirming youth group called—"

My mother intercepted, "Finding a church community is so important for a young couple. It's the foundation of the family, isn't it? The first thing Butch and I did when we got married was join Redeemer, and we've been so blessed to have Jonathan receive a sound Biblical education there."

"Yes, I agree, but—"

Mom interrupted Dawn by holding out the plate of bars to her.

"Oh, thank you, Linda."

Mom nodded and put the plate back on the tray. She didn't know Dawn. It would take more than lemon bars to redirect her.

"But it's incredibly important to find a church where every member of the family feels loved and accepted." Dawn patted her lips with a napkin and took a sip of tea. "Don't you agree?"

I had been reduced to a spectator at the politest soccer game ever, only instead of a ball, Dawn and my mother were passing lemon bars and blocking theology. The score appeared to be tied.

"Yes, I do agree with that," Mom said.

Advantage Dawn. I took a bar for the simple reason that eating it hid my grin.

"Has Jonathan ever told you the story of how I came to know Christ?" Dawn asked.

My mother leaned forward in the recliner and shook her head. "No, please tell me."

Dawn took a deep breath. "I grew up on the Mille Lacs Band of Ojibwe Reservation. My family is traditional and keeps with the ways of my people. I love them and respect their beliefs, but I always yearned for something…well, something different. So when I was old enough, I went to the University of Minnesota to study wildlife preservation. The summer between my junior and senior year, I took an internship studying the loon population at Spirit Lake. I didn't even know the loons shared the lake with a bunch of campers!"

Mom and I laughed, but Dawn drove toward the goal.

"It was just for a summer, mind you. An internship. Nothing more. But I returned to school with a hole inside me.

The longer I lived with that ache, the more certain I was that the people from the camp had something I needed, so one night I left home and drove back to Spirit Lake. To Paul and Hannah, who led me to Christ."

"Oh, Dawn, that's lovely." Mom's eyes filled with tears.

Mine did too, but for different reasons. Unlike me, Mom didn't know the part that came next.

"It was the best decision I've ever made, Linda. I just wish it hadn't cost me my relationship with my mother."

Mom blinked and reached for the arm of her chair. "What do you mean? Your mother rejected you for giving your life to Christ?"

Dawn's eyes narrowed, aiming for the goal. "She rejected me for choosing a life different from the one she wanted me to live."

It was nothing but net.

"I'm so sorry." Mom's voice trembled.

"I am too, but the experience has given me a heart for kids at risk. In fact, I work with the youth group at One Heart. ABLAZE is an awesome bunch of kids of all races, sexual orientations and identities, ability, and economic levels. Everyone is on fire for God, and no one judges. Linda, it would be a place where Jonathan would be accepted without reservation. We meet every Wednesday night, and I'd be happy to pick him up and drop him off, if it's all right with you."

It took a moment for that to sink in. Accepted without reservation. What would that even feel like?

"Oh my, Dawn, how kind of you to think of Jonathan." Mom dusted the powdered sugar off her pants and picked up the tray with the empty plate and glasses.

Was it possible? Had Dawn reached my mother? Of course she had. She was Dawn.

Mom continued, "Thank you so much for the invitation,

but I'm afraid we couldn't ask you to do that. Such a big time commitment and, after all, we are all very happy at Redeemer. Isn't that right, Jonathan?"

Damn, talk about the most subtle feint of all. "Right," I said. "Sure."

Mom stood and walked toward the foyer. Dawn followed her, pausing to glance back at me before she left.

Game over.

CHAPTER NINETEEN

Ooh! And then there are so many great quotes in *Doctor Who*! There was—" Sketch's enthusiasm was a bit much at 6:30 a.m. on a Monday morning after a craptastic weekend. Ian had continued to text me weather reports for Southern states, and I had continued to ignore his texts. Mom had informed me that she had made an appointment for us at Deliverance Clinic, but (and this was the lone high point) it was for two months out. *They must be good to be so busy,* she'd said as she dove back into a book titled *How to Raise a Man of God.*

Like I said, craptastic weekend.

"As impressive as it is that you possess an encyclopedic knowledge of *Doctor Who,* I still say we should go with *Being gay isn't a choice, but being homophobic is,*" Mason argued.

"We need to be clever!" Sketch insisted.

"We need to be clear!" Mason countered, but he wrote *Doctor Who* on the white board in the art classroom anyway. It joined *Star Trek, Star Wars, Buffy the Vampire Slayer,* and *X-Files.*

"IT DOES NOT MATTER!" I said because a) it is a known fact that I am not a morning person, and b) someone needed to stop the insanity. "Get real! Whether we go with sci-fi quotes or not, the truth is that these posters are going to stay up for about five seconds before someone rips them down. None of this matters."

"That's it! Jonathan, you're brilliant!" Sketch ran over and squeezed me until my ribs hurt. Mason and I looked at her like she'd just lost the last bit of her mind. "Don't you see?" She bounced, looking like a much younger version of Enid. "We make double layer posters. On the front we have an attention-grabbing sci-fi quote with the details of our first GSA meeting on normal copy paper. Then, WHEN it gets ripped off there's another *laminated* poster behind it that states *Being gay isn't a choice, but being homophobic is!* Of course it would have the details about the first meeting as well."

Mason and I sat in awe of Sketch. Her brilliance knew no bounds.

❖

The posters were a hit. By Tuesday afternoon, every hallway and classroom had a laminated poster informing the entire school body and faculty that homophobia is a choice and that the first eBay GSA meeting was going to be held after school in the art room. I even saw some crumpled sci-fi posters smoothed out and rehung around the school.

"This is so exciting!" Simon wheeled down the hallway toward the office where he needed to sign in and pick up his visitor badge. I walked next to him, carrying the huge sheet cake I had discovered in the back of his van.

"This is really nice, Simon, but I don't think the four of us can eat this much."

"Have a little faith, Jonathan! People will come."

I fought the urge to tell him that the days when he and

I had sat at the shore of Spirit Lake, talking about God's unconditional love, felt long gone. A little faith was a lot to ask.

"We'll see." I pushed the button for the elevator that would take Simon to the lower level of the school.

My cell pinged in the elevator. I pulled it out and read the text from Ian. *92 degrees with slightly overcast clouds in Los Angeles. C'mon, Jonathan. Think about it.* I grimaced and shoved my cell back in my pocket.

"Everything okay?" Simon grabbed the arms of his wheelchair as we lurched to a stop.

"Yeah, I think so. It's Ian. He's, well, he's—" How could I explain Ian to Simon when I didn't understand what was going on with him myself?

"Everything okay with you two?"

"Yeah, it's just the distance. It's hard."

"Of course it is," Simon said.

"And sometimes it feels like he's—" Again, I had no clue how to finish my sentence.

"Like he's what?"

"Like he's lost touch with reality," I blurted, hating myself for saying it aloud.

"I imagine that's tempting for him right now."

"What do you mean? *Tempting for him right now?*" I held the door of the elevator as he wheeled himself out so I didn't get to see his face when he stammered and coughed into his sleeve.

"This way to the art room?" He looked down the hallway.

I stepped in front of him, blocking his view. "Simon, is something wrong with Ian? Have you talked to him?"

He looked at his feet perched on the wheelchair's

footrests, the spiderweb in the corner, the grimy metal door of the boiler room. "Oh, he called me the other day, but no. Nothing's wrong, Jonathan. Ian's fine. He's just fine."

I was about to ask for a definition of *fine* when the door to the art room opened, and Ms. Owens came out, her face flushed.

"Oh my, Mr. Fletcher, I'm so pleased to meet you! I've admired your work for years!" Ms. Owens stuck a pencil in her hair and held the door.

"Please call me Simon, and I'd love to have you come visit my new studio, Young at Art. You're welcome anytime." Simon wheeled into the art room.

"I thought your studio was in Duluth." Ms. Owens trailed behind him.

"It was, but my fiancée and I felt led to the Twin Cities, so here we are. We officially open next week, but please do come see the studio any time."

"I will!" Ms. Owens practically floated over to help Sketch move the chairs into a circle.

"Fiancée?" I grinned at Simon.

"That's not official yet either." He pulled a small black velvet box out of his coat pocket. Inside was a ring of two entwined tree branches, one white gold and one yellow gold, with dozens of delicate leaves that nestled little diamonds. A one-of-a-kind, just like its designer. "Think she'll like it?"

"She's going to love it. When are you going to ask her?"

"Tonight. If I don't chicken out again. I've been trying to screw up the courage all week." Simon grimaced and put the ring back in his coat pocket.

All the talk about proposals had distracted me from the fact that the art room was filling up with people. I'd seen Ms. Jennings walk in and sit by Ms. Owens. That hadn't surprised me, but I couldn't believe it when a bunch of kids, all wearing

Doctor Who T-shirts, arrived and headed for the cake. Sketch gave them each two slices. In retrospect, that was probably a mistake, but how could she have known that half the jazz band, the entire chess team, and an odd assortment of random individuals were also planning on coming?

"Who are all these people?" I asked Mason who was muttering numbers and tapping the air with his pointer finger. "And why have I never seen them before?"

The look he gave me shut me up. "We need more chairs. Tell Sketch to cut the cake slices in half."

"Done," I said as he bolted out of the room.

❖

"So, um, hello." Sketch stood up. "Welcome to eBay's GSA!"

Long, awkward pause.

She blushed and sat back down.

Simon cleared his throat. "My name is Simon Fletcher. I am not a teacher at this school, nor am I gay; however, I am an ally, and I am honored to be the advisor at the first ever Gay-Straight Alliance at East Bay Christian Academy." Sketch looked like she could kiss Simon for bailing her out. "What is important to know is that you don't need to be gay to be part of this club. You just need to care that all students, gay and straight, are safe within these walls."

I sat there, the hard core inside me clenching against his easy words and belief that things could change. He didn't know my team was practicing for the game against Sacred Heart without me. My calves ached. My thighs tightened. My mouth flooded with the flavor of urinal cake.

"Why don't we go around the room and introduce ourselves? Feel free to tell as much or as little about yourself as you'd like with the full knowledge that whatever is said here, stays here."

Simon looked at me, as I knew he would, but I shook my head. He turned to Mason.

"Hi, my name is Mason. I'm gay, but that's probably the least interesting thing about me. What you need to know about me, and this is for real, is that I'm going to win *Project Runway* someday." And just like that, Mason made it okay for people to talk. Jessica, the girl who played saxophone in the jazz band, blushed as she introduced us to her girlfriend. Nick, the captain of the chess team, winked at Mason. I shifted in my chair and frowned. One of the kids in a Doctor Who T-shirt named Henry admitted that he came because he thought we were forming a sci-fi club, but said he would come again because we seemed cool. The circle caught up with Sketch, founder of it all, and even I leaned forward to hear what she had to say.

"My name is Frances, but I don't like that name. Just like I don't like being called *she* or *her*. Most people think I go by Sketch because I like to draw and paint, but really, I call myself that because that's what I feel like, an outline that was more true before someone colored me pink. Am I a lesbian? Maybe. Girl parts are prettier than boy parts, that's for sure. But it goes deeper than that, and I just don't know what else to say except that I'm Sketch, and it's freaking awesome that you all came today."

And then it was my turn to talk.

I stared at my tennis shoes. Three black stripes on leather, the white streaked by grass and dirt smudges that would never come out, no matter how hard I scrubbed.

"My name is Jonathan Cooper. I'm here because..." I thought about the way that sentence should end if I weren't so damn afraid: *because I'm gay.* But there was no coming back from words like that. "I'm here because I want to make this a safer school for everyone," I said and told myself it was true.

"You're here for school safety?" Jessica, the saxophone player looked confused. "I thought—"

"You thought wrong," I answered her unasked question and glanced toward Simon, half expecting to catch him frowning at me. But he smiled at me and dipped his chin. He understood. I wasn't ready to let people, not even the members of the GSA, see my real face.

Chapter Twenty

The first thing we need to do is organize a fund-raiser. Does anybody have any ideas?" Sketch had found her voice, thanks to Simon breaking the ice, and now there was no shutting her up. "You know, for printing costs for flyers and maybe even a banner for pep fests. Things like that. Eventually, I want to bring in speakers to talk to the school about sexual orientation and gender identities and how we can become a more affirming community. All those things cost money. I thought we could start by selling cookies."

"I am not going around this school hawking Thin Mints like a friggin' Girl Scout," Nick, the captain of the chess club, said.

"We could sell Samoas. Those are my favorite." Jessica, the saxophone player, reached for her girlfriend's hand.

"Let me clarify. I AM NOT SELLING ANY COOKIES." Nick leaned back in his chair and glared at Jessica.

Simon jumped in before things boiled over. "Sketch has a great vision for this club, but she's right. We're going to need to come up with some money. Does anybody else have any ideas?"

"We're the eBay GSA," Mason said. "So why don't we act like eBay and have an auction? We could all donate a few things, and kids in school could bid on them. Highest bid gets the item."

Simon leaned forward. "What kind of items are you talking about, Mason?"

"That's just it; it doesn't have to be stuff. I mean, it could be anything. Like Jonathan could offer to take someone's senior pictures. Sketch could auction off her *Dying Dove* painting. Nick, you could sell chess lessons. I bet Jessica could give music lessons. We could auction off other things too. Like raking leaves or washing cars or cleaning houses."

"That's a great idea, Mason!" Simon leaned back and tapped his fingers, which I knew meant he was pumped. "You can count on me to auction one of my sculptures."

Sketch's mouth fell open. "Simon, that's huge. I mean, you don't need to do that! You're a professional artist!"

"Happy to do it, Sketch."

"And you can use any art supplies you need from the art room." Ms. Owens smiled at Sketch. "I want to offer all the support I can. Really, I do."

"Same offer from the science classroom. If you need any dissected frogs, they're yours." Ms. Jennings winked.

"Thank you, ladies. Now, about this auction. How are we going to reach our buyers?" Simon looked around the circle.

"Again, we imitate eBay," Mason said. "I can design a website where we'll list all the items. We can have people place their bids right online, and we can announce the winners at the homecoming dance!"

"Perfect. Send me the link when you have it, and I'll promote it on the Young at Art website too. In the meantime, everybody think about what you can donate. Think outside the box, people. Let's raise some money and make this school a safer place for every student!"

You know the saying you can take the counselor out of

camp, but you can't take the camp out of the counselor? Well, it's true. Before Simon was done talking, I could almost see the branches of the willow tree swaying in the breeze down at the edge of Spirit Lake.

"What are you going to sell in the auction?" I asked Mason as we stacked chairs after the meeting.

"What else? A one of a kind haute couture prom dress to be designed and sewn by none other than yours truly! Très chic!" Mason looked so pleased I hated to tell him that he'd be lucky to get a five-dollar bid.

Of course, he didn't get *a* five-dollar bid. The first day the website went live, he got *seven* of them. Then he got a ten-dollar bid, followed by a twenty-dollar bid, which was blown out of the water by a thirty-dollar bid until he was almost impossible to be around. He checked the bid status with the fervor of a Wall Street market analyst.

"I'm up to forty-five dollars! That's the highest bid in the whole auction except for Simon's sculpture!" He squealed, and by *squealed,* I mean high-pitched sound vibrations that made me want to stick chopsticks through my eardrums. "Your photo shoot is up to seventeen fifty," he said with a smile.

"Bite me." This snarky comeback earned me a whole thirty seconds of silence as we walked to American lit on Friday.

"So, do you know yet what you're going to write your essay about?" Mason asked me as we walked into Gilchrist's classroom.

"No clue. You?"

"Yeah, that the real sinners were the Puritans. The women hated Hester Prynne because she was prettier than they were. The men wanted to bone her themselves." Mason raised his eyebrow high above his tortoiseshell glasses and smirked. "Talk about the sin of coveting! What's that compared to a little pickle tickle in the woods?"

I laughed. How couldn't I? The more I got to know Mason, as irritating as he sometimes could be, the more I wanted to get to know him. It was a fact that disturbed me on many levels.

"Technically," I pointed out, "what Dimmesdale and Hester did together was adultery."

Mason sighed as he sat next to me in the front row. "Loving someone is not a sin, Jonathan. When are you going to believe that?"

In a classroom full of mumbling voices not yet hushed by Mr. Gilchrist, I alone was silent.

Chapter Twenty-one

Homecoming week.

Pajama day. Tie-dye day. School spirit day where the only thing I had to wear was my soccer jersey and a pair of jeans. A pep fest where Coach Thomas and my team paraded around the gym without me. Could it have been any worse?

The answer is yes. Yes, it could.

It got worse when Sketch set up a table in the cafeteria where she insisted we sit during lunch so we could field questions about the GSA and the fund-raiser. I let Mason and Sketch do most of the talking and buried my head in *The Scarlet Letter*. I managed to accomplish two things. I avoided all the looks of disgust from the table near the window, and I finished the book. Two weeks past due, but better late than never. It was Wednesday of homecoming week, and I was three pages away from the ending when my cell phone vibrated in my pocket. It was Ian.

Hey, I hope you don't have plans for Friday night.

This was ridiculous. Now he was planning a specific date for us to run away? I hit the reply button. *I am not running away with you. I've already told you that.*

He replied right away. *I know that. I've given up on that idea, but here's the thing. There's a conference this weekend at the U of M. Bovine Basics 101. Stupid, right? But I told the Hun and Castro that I want to be a dairy farmer and they said I could go!*

I couldn't believe my eyes. Ian was coming to Minnesota.

Friday? As in Friday the night of the homecoming dance, which I was pretty certain Mason thought we were going to together?

It's homecoming this week, I texted.

Ping! Man, he was fast today. *Awesome! If you'll get over being an uptight douche, we can go to the dance together.*

Yeah, sometimes life is a surprising son of a bitch and you find yourself sitting in the cafeteria in your pajamas, trying to decide if you've just been asked out or insulted.

By Thursday, the only thing that mattered was that Ian was coming for a visit. Not that he had been pushing me to run away with him for over a month. Not that he'd called me an uptight douche. Not even the look on Mason's face when I told him I was going to the dance with Ian. Sure, he said he understood. With his words at least.

No, the only thing that mattered was making the weekend with Ian perfect. Romantic, even. One problem, though. I didn't know squat about being romantic.

"You've got to have wine." Sketch handed me a bottle and a corkscrew. We were sitting in my car in the parking lot of the school early Friday morning. I didn't even want to think about how many school rules I was breaking.

"You took this from your parents' wine cellar? Won't they notice?"

"Yes, Jonathan, they're absolutely going to realize this one bottle is missing from the five hundred or so other bottles they have. I will be grounded for life, and it will be ALL YOUR FAULT." Melodramatic, much?

"I don't know," I said, remembering Ian's crack at the bonfire about wishing they'd served beer at the last supper. "I'm not sure he even likes wine."

"Fine. Serve him Mountain Dew, then. That will be *so* romantic." Sketch tried to take the bottle back.

"No, wait." I squinted at the fine print on the back of the label. "Pinot grigio? Does that go with pie?"

"How the hell should I know? You asked me to help you be romantic. I didn't know I had to be a freaking sommelier!"

"A someofawhat?"

"Nothing." She laugh-snorted a puff of smoke into the cold air inside my car. "Listen, Jonathan, wine is romantic. I don't think it matters what kind. Though, pie? For real? You should have chocolate mousse."

"No, it has to be pie," I insisted, remembering the day Ian had raided the kitchen at Spirit Lake Bible Camp and we had spent the afternoon gorging ourselves on pie and kisses up at Porcupine Point. "Strawberry rhubarb, actually."

Sketch grunted. "Fine. Suit yourself."

Other memories from camp surfaced after school as I took my second shower for the day, scrubbing every inch of my body, which grew harder with each blast of hot water and each second that brought me closer to Ian. I thought of him when I ran my razor over my cheeks, and later, when I snuck into the downstairs bathroom and dug through Mom's assortment of pill bottles until I found Dad's aftershave.

"Are you wearing cologne?" Mom put down her book *From Sinner to Saint* and sniffed the air when I walked into the living room, my backpack dangling from my right hand.

"No," I lied. "New shampoo. It's scented."

It was a night of lies. Lots and lots of lies.

"It's nice. You're taking your backpack to homecoming?" Mom asked.

"Yeah, I'm bringing a blanket in case, you know, it gets cold." The forecast called for frost, but it was still a lie unless a dish towel wrapped around two wine glasses could be considered a blanket. As lies went, it was a small one.

"You wouldn't be cold if you were playing."

"Mom, don't start." I slung the backpack over my shoulder. She turned her head slightly at the clinking sound. "There's a dance afterward so I'll be home late. You don't need to stay up for me."

She nodded, picked up her book, and said nothing. It was almost too easy.

Of course something had to go wrong. It was bound to with that many lies and laws being broken. I just didn't expect it to involve pie.

"I'm sorry, but we're all out." The lady behind the counter at the bakery on 43rd and Nicollet shook her head.

"You can't be. You don't understand. I've got to have strawberry rhubarb!"

"Sorry, kid. I've got some real nice apple pies. Fresh from the oven."

In the end, I settled for caramel apple and stashed it in the backseat while I drove into downtown Minneapolis, my stomach clenching and flipping with each mile that brought me closer to him.

I briefly wondered what Ian told Matilda the Hun and Fidel Castro about how he was getting from the Greyhound bus station to the University of Minnesota as I parked the car and stood outside, scanning faces while my heart thudded in my chest.

Some lie. A good one, knowing Ian.

And then it didn't matter because a silver bus, Number 320, pulled in, its brakes squeaking into the brisk night air. Then the doors opened and there he was, walking down the steps and looking around for me. Duffel bag in one hand, red curls poking out from under his baseball cap, folded journal sticking out of his back pocket. Three months a stranger to me, I would have known him anywhere. Ian.

"Hey," I called out, my voice catching. "Over here."

He ran into my arms, his body slamming into mine. "Hey, yourself!" He breathed into the nape of my neck, hot against my cool skin, while my pulse tripped like a rap song beneath his mouth.

We kissed in my car until the windows fogged up and I had to turn on the defrost.

We kissed in the parking lot at the U of M.

We kissed in the boys' bathroom of Comstock Hall because it's a long ride from Wisconsin to Minnesota and Ian had drunk two liters of Mountain Dew to stay awake.

We lied and told the guy at the front desk that I was his brother, helping him move into the dorm. I even carried his duffel bag to add to the illusion. We almost blew it when Ian grabbed my hand as we walked down the hallway toward his room. I yanked back and shot a glance at the open doors where college kids studied or lounged in their rooms.

The dorm room was far from romantic. A bunk bed complete with plastic mattresses hogged most of the space. A tiny closet was inset into the concrete walls that had yellowed and chipped over the years. One desk under a window with bent aluminum blinds was the only other piece of furniture.

We didn't know how long it would be before his roommate—Robert Atkins from Crookston, according to Ian's welcome packet—arrived. It could have been minutes. It could have been hours. I wish I could tell you that was the only reason Ian pushed me onto the bottom bunk and crawled on top of me before the door to his dorm had even closed behind us, but that would be another lie.

"I brought wine." I sat up, reached for my backpack, which I had laid on the desk, and pulled out the bottle and corkscrew.

"Sweet!" He took it out of my hand.

"Actually, I think it's dry."

Ian plunged the corkscrew into the cork. "What else did you bring?"

"Glasses," I said as he took a drink from the bottle. "And pie." I reached across the bed for the square white pastry box on the desk. Ian smiled, remembering. "I tried to find strawberry rhubarb, but they were sold out. I bought caramel apple."

Ian opened the box and inhaled. "That's okay. We can do all sorts of things with caramel." He dipped his finger in the sticky mess and raised it to my lips. "Now close your eyes," he whispered, continuing the game we had played at Porcupine Point where he had tricked me into kissing him by making me close my eyes.

I shook my head and kept my eyes fixed on his face. Same freckles. Same killer eyes. Same musky scent that came off his skin and left me dizzy.

"No?" He blinked.

"No." I took the bottle from him and held it to my lips. The wine hit my mouth and slid down my throat, cold and wet, and afterward, I was thirstier than ever. "I...I want to watch."

"Fucking A, who are you and what have you done with my boyfriend?" Ian laughed. "I may have to enroll in the whole damn junior dairy farmer program."

A future of weekends with Ian. Was it possible? I lifted the bottle to my lips and drank until my head spun and my fingertips tingled.

"Now come here." He took the bottle and put it on the desk next to the bed. He wrapped his arms around my waist and slid his hand down my stomach and lower. "I've been wanting to do this for so long."

I inhaled sharply.

"What's wrong?" he asked me.

"Nothing. It's just—" I shook my head, unable to find a word that meant too fast, too much, too slow, too little all at once. I lay back on the plastic mattress, and Ian climbed on top of me. He must have bumped the wine bottle because it smashed to the floor.

"Do you want to do this?" he asked.

"I don't know," I lied, a whopper of a lie that grew stronger and bigger and harder with each tug of a zipper, each awkward fumble with boxers and jeans and lubricant and condoms. Yes, lubricant and condoms. While I had brought pie and wine, Ian had brought lubricant and condoms.

Ian, naked, was even more beautiful than I remembered. Maybe not David Beckham beautiful, but real with his farmer tan and freckles, not some poster that hung over my bed and provided occasional inspiration. I traced my fingers along the thinness of him, in and out of the indentations of his collarbone, down his sternum, across his ribs until he squirmed and shouted *No fair!* and pinned my hands above my head so I couldn't tickle him anymore. If possible, he was even thinner than he'd been last summer. I closed my eyes and leaned toward him.

He pressed his lips to mine until there was no thought, no question, no sound, no objection. There was only Ian and the smell of his skin, the softness of his lips, the sharpness of his hipbone as it cut into my thigh.

"Do you want me to stop, Jonathan?" he whispered when he put his hands on my shoulders and turned me gently.

"Don't you dare stop," I said, lifting my hips for him.

If Ian said anything after that, I don't know. My world

narrowed until the only real things in it were pain and pleasure and sweat and a hot plastic mattress.

Then he came, sprawled across my back and panting, and afterward we gambled on five more minutes.

"Let's skip the dance," I said, as we lay, a half-eaten pie perched on my stomach, on a mattress covered in crumbs and caramel and the faint splatter of wine. "We could stay here all night. I probably don't have to be home until two a.m."

"Skip the dance? Are you crazy?" He untangled himself and tiptoed over the puddle of wine and broken bits of bottle. "I've been looking forward to seeing your fancy school and hanging out with the guys on your—Shit!" He pulled a shard of glass out of his foot. "On your soccer team. Or don't you want to go?"

Ian's unspoken question hung in the space between us. *Or don't you want them to meet me?*

It hung next to all the secrets I'd kept from him: the fact that I was still hiding who I was at school…the guys he'd told me to wreck had been my friends…I wasn't even on the soccer team anymore. "Of course I do." I climbed off the bed, jerked on my jeans, and winced. "Let's go."

Like I said. It was a night of lies.

Chapter Twenty-two

I'm going to dance with you." Ian's hand started at my knee and moved up my leg, making my driving less than perfect as we left the U of M campus and headed toward Minnetonka. "In front of everybody."

"You're crazy!" I said. "This is a homecoming dance at my school, not some gay bar."

"Do you really think I came here because I'm dying to sit through endless hours of cow lectures? If we're going to a dance, we're going to dance together!"

"You're tipsy!"

"And you're hot!" He reached his goal and squeezed. The car swerved.

"All right. One dance!" I gave in before I crashed Dad's car.

I heard the music blasting inside the gymnasium the minute we walked in the front door of the school. A slow song. Wonderful.

"C'mon, Jonathan!" Ian looked toward the gym where kids dance-groped while clueless chaperones sipped punch and chatted with each other.

A prickling feeling crept over my skin, and I turned to see Pete, Luke, and Brandon come out of the boys' bathroom.

"This was a bad idea. I think we should leave."

"And go where? Back to the dorm so we can play Pictionary with Robert Atkins?" he teased me.

"No, but we should still leave."

"We could go back to your place. You could introduce me to your mom."

I drew a picture of that in my mind. Mom, Ian, and me sitting around the living room. *Hello, Mom, I'd like you to meet my boyfriend.* "Ah, that would be a no."

"Exactly. So dance with me, Jonathan." Ian grabbed my hand and pulled me toward the gym.

Pete walked right for us, Brandon and Luke trailing behind him. "Jonathan Cooper, holding hands with his boyfriend? Guys, can you believe this bullshit? The school is being taken over by a bunch of fags!"

I yanked my hand back and shoved it in my pocket.

Ian stiffened and turned to look at me, the same hard glint in his eyes as the night at Porcupine Point when he'd sworn he'd never let anyone make him feel small and vulnerable and ashamed again.

He started to move.

I grabbed his arm. "No, Ian. It's not worth it."

"Since when?" He yanked his arm out of my grasp and headed for Pete.

SHIT! I spun in a circle in the hallway, searching for anyone to help. Mason, Sketch, Simon, a certified bomb defuser. Hell, even Principal Hardin. I spotted Mason and Sketch inside the gym by the podium. They were positioning her *Dying Dove* portrait on an easel. Ms. Owens was drooling over Simon's sculpture. No Principal Hardin. No bomb defuser either. So much for backup.

"Ian, stop!" I shouted, but of course he didn't. He barged

right up to them. Luke moved to the right. Brandon stepped to the left. I recognized the formation, but Ian didn't.

Shit, shit, shit, shit, SHIT! I barely noticed that the music had stopped.

"Can I have your attention?" Sketch's amplified voice blasted from inside the gym.

I looked through the open doors and saw Sketch standing behind the podium. The auction had begun, which meant that no one would be coming out into the hallway for a while.

"As many of you know, we recently started a new club in school. The eBay GSA!" Sketch fist pumped the air.

I moved toward Ian, who was surrounded and didn't even know it. Luke stepped in front of me. I moved right. Luke lunged. I broke left and burst between Ian and Pete.

"The first item in our auction is a one-of-a-kind prom creation by our very own fashion forward, Mason! Our highest bidder, going for one hundred and fifty dollars, is Jenna Stevens!" Applause thundered inside the gym.

"Nice move." Pete took a step forward and laid his hand on my chest. "But then again, your whole life has been one big feint, hasn't it, Jonathan?" He shoved and I stumbled into Ian's arms.

"The second item up for auction is a Star Wars collectible card signed by George Lucas! And the highest bidder is—"

"Get out of here, Jonathan." Ian spun me toward the front door and reached into his pocket.

"The third item up for auction is a sculpture by renowned artist and GSA advisor, Simon Fletcher." The oohs and aahs told me the auction was a hit.

Just like the front door and me. If anyone had glanced into the hallway, that's what they would have seen. Me tripping and bouncing off the front door. They wouldn't have seen the real action. They wouldn't have seen the wall of bodies surrounding the short redheaded boy, an unknown stranger, who pressed his straight razor against the soccer captain's neck. They wouldn't have noticed the look on the redheaded boy's face. Hard and chiseled. Just like Simon's sculpture that, according to Sketch, had sold for five hundred dollars to Ms. Caroline Owens.

Brandon and Luke closed in on Ian.

"Tell them to back off," Ian commanded Pete in a voice that was calm. Too calm.

"Fuck you." Defiance flashed in Pete's eyes. It almost hid the fear.

"You'd like to fuck me, wouldn't you?" Ian reached down with his other hand and grabbed Pete's crotch. "Yeah, I thought as much." Ian pressed the blade farther into Pete's neck. Drops of blood trickled down his neck and spilled over the white EB letters on the blue jacket. "The worst haters are usually just too afraid to step out of their own closets."

I stepped past Brandon and grabbed Ian's arm. "That's enough! Let him go!"

He turned to look me in the eye. "I told you, Jonathan. You have to wreck 'em. Crush 'em into scrap metal. Don't you get it?" The muscles of his jaw twitched.

"No, I don't! What the hell are you doing with that razor?"

He blinked, lowered the blade, and took a step backward.

Pete exhaled, reached to cover the bulge in his pants, and hobbled away toward the bathroom with as much dignity as a guy with a full boner could summon. Brandon and Luke stared after him, but they scurried into the gym when Ian flicked the blade in their direction.

"He's the one who sent that picture of you all around school, isn't he?"

"Yeah, probably. Though it was Luke who gave it to him."

"Why did you stop me? I was trying to help you!" In and out. In and out, Ian played with the razor.

The auction ended and people moved toward the gym doors.

"By bringing a blade into my school? Sounds more like a way to get me expelled."

"Fine." Ian closed the razor and shoved it in his pocket.

"I thought you threw that off the cliff at Porcupine Point!"

"Correction, I threw my old man's razor off the cliff at Porcupine Point. This one is mine." He patted his pocket and glared at Pete, who came out of the bathroom, leaned against a locker, and pressed a bit of toilet paper against his neck.

"You got to wreck 'em before they can wreck you." His face hardened.

"Hey." I touched his arm. "I thought you wanted to dance."

CHAPTER TWENTY-THREE

Everything is black. Black like ebony. It doesn't matter if my eyes are open or shut. I'm guessing it's late. Maybe two a.m. I have no idea.

"Grace?" My voice echoes in the room like a hollow thing.

The darkness shifts into shadows like one of my black-and-white photographs as my eyes adjust. Shapes emerge. The closet. The empty chair where Grace belongs.

A shadow steps away from the wall. "Grace?" I say again. "Is that you?" But I know it's not. The shape is wrong. Too tall. Too big. Too blue. It registers. The fact that I've begun to see color. I take a deep, gulping breath.

He crosses the room in four heavy strides, his shoes thwapping hard on the floor. I hear the clink of rattling metal, the crackle of electronic static. I close my eyes and try to hear the music again.

As defenses go, denial sucks.

"Searching for Grace? Looks like she's deserted you."

"No." I scan the shadows of the room. "She wouldn't do that."

"Then where is she? It's just you and me here, kid." The stink of him slaps me across the face. I try to roll on my side. Try to rock to the rhythm of the music, but he grabs my shoulder and forces me to face him. He leans over me, his sweat dripping onto my face. "Look at me!" he spits.

I open my eyes. Wipe away his sweat, his spit, my tears. "What do you want from me?" I ask.

"Just a little thing called the truth, and I'm not going anywhere 'til I get it," he promises.

God help me, I believe him.

I squeeze my eyes tight and pray for a miracle. The door creaks open, and I hear her voice, raspy but strong, booming in the room.

"Out!" She fires the word into the room like a cannon. "You get out and stay out until I say you can come in here!"

Then all I hear is her panting fury, his heavy footsteps as he crosses the room, the swoosh of the door opening and closing. I still wait, eyes clenched shut in the aftermath of silence, just to be sure, and count. One...two...three...

"You're safe, Jonathan. I'm here." Her voice is ancient. As if she were around when time itself was born. I peer into the shadows of dove gray and charcoal and wonder why they ever frightened me at all. But of course, I know. It's because he was here. Looming over everything.

"He's never going to give up," I whisper. Grace, standing next to my bed, nods and puts her hand on mine. The warmth of her touch travels through my skin, up my arm, across my chest until it takes root in my heart.

"Yes, I'm afraid that's true." Her sigh is a hard thing that sticks in her throat. "Soon, very soon, you're going to have to face what happened."

"I can't, Grace! You know that!"

"Hush!" She clacks her teeth. "Don't you tell me what I know, impertinent child. Here's what *I know*. This life doesn't give you much choice about the troubles that come your way. They come and you face them when they do. Simple as that."

"There's nothing simple about that." I risk impertinence again, but she hushes me.

"Course there is. All you gotta choose is what face you wear when you stare those troubles down. Your real face or some mask. Now, that's enough. The time for talking is past. This time is for resting, what precious little you have left of it." She leans down and kisses my forehead. Her breath is a breeze blowing through a forest of birch and fir.

I stifle a yawn. "Will you stay with me?"

"Certainly." She settles in the chair beside my bed.

"And will you be there in the morning?"

"Don't you doubt it, sweet Jonathan. Not for one little second." Back and forth she rocks; the creaking of the chair and the sound of her humming are the last things I hear as I drift off to sleep.

CHAPTER TWENTY-FOUR

Where are we going? I thought we were going to dance?" Ian asked as I walked away from the gym.

"We are. In the art room."

"Why not in the gym?" Ian looked in at the couples on the dance floor.

"Because we can't." I walked farther down the hallway.

"Don't you mean *you* can't?"

"Please, Ian, I don't want to fight. I—"

"Ian McGuire! I heard you were in town studying the differences between Guernsey and Holstein cows!" Simon wheeled out of the gym. I knew he'd want to say hello to Ian, but his timing couldn't have been worse. *Project Get Ian Away from Pete* was almost complete.

Ian shot a look of triumph at me and walked to Simon. "Close, but not quite. I believe tomorrow we are learning how to overcome the challenges of alfalfa winterkill. It's scintillating stuff, I'm telling you."

"Sounds like it." Simon's face grew serious. "And everything else?"

"It's official."

"I'm so sorry, Ian."

I understood Ian and Simon's conversation about as much

as I understood the challenges of alfalfa winterkill. Which was not at all.

"Okay, I give. What's up?" I asked.

"Nothing. Just stupid stuff." Ian looked away from me.

Simon dipped his chin and said nothing.

"Jonathan was just about to show me the art room. How about we catch up later?" And with that, Ian slammed the lid on the so-called stupid stuff.

"Sure. I'll be popping wheelies on the dance floor. Feel free to save me from completely embarrassing myself." Simon grinned and wheeled back into the gym.

"Care to tell me what that was all about?" I asked as we walked down the stairs to the lower level of the school.

"Not really."

"C'mon, talk to me," I pushed.

"Drop it, Jonathan."

I did because a) Ian looked about as talkative as a Guernsey cow choking on alfalfa, and b) we had reached the art room.

"Here it is, where all the magic happens." I held the door open. Ian walked up to the mannequins I had staged in the center of the red light district.

"Okay, I get the paint and canvases, but what do these two have to do with art, and why are they wearing crowns?"

I started to tell him about how I've been studying Robert Mapplethorpe's techniques with *Two Men Dancing*, but he left me standing by the mannequins and wandered over to the radio on Ms. Owens's desk. He fiddled until he found a station that was playing a slow song.

"So this is supposed to be like the photo of two guys dancing that you sent me?" He walked over to one of the mannequins, took a crown from its head, and slipped it on. "The one where they're wearing crowns?"

"Yeah, that's the one."

He removed the other crown and held it out to me. "I thought they were naked."

"They were," I said, slipping on the crown and feeling totally stupid, "but it didn't work when I photographed them in black and white. Mason suggested I try some color to make them feel more alive."

"Mason?" Ian scrunched his eyebrows and cocked his head.

"Just a guy in my art class." I changed the subject. "Ian, what happened upstairs, that wasn't cool."

"Agreed. What did that guy letter in? Being an asshole?" He held his arms out.

"Actually, he lettered in soccer." I stepped into them. He pressed against me. Electricity arced between us, and I felt the familiar burn every place our bodies touched.

"You're shitting me. That guy's your teammate?"

I followed his lead and swayed left. "He was my captain. He was my best friend."

Ian pulled away. "Was? Jonathan, what's been going on?"

"Nothing." I pulled him back into my arms. "Just dance with me."

He adjusted his crown. "Okay, we'll dance just like the guys in your picture. There's only one problem."

"Which is?"

"They were naked." Ian reached for the top button on his shirt.

"No way!" I twirled us, too fast for the music, but I didn't care. Ian laughed and pulled me close. His hand traveled down the small of my back. We stopped moving and stood there, staring at each other in our costume crowns.

"I've missed this," I whispered.

"Funny, but I don't recall us ever dancing in crowns before."

"Not *this* exactly. You. I've missed you."

He leaned toward me, his eyes closing. His lips opening.

"You two make me want to puke." Pete's voice snapped me out of the Ian-haze that had wrapped around me. I stepped out of Ian's arms and looked toward the doorway where Pete stood, a baseball bat in one hand.

"The feeling is mutual." Ian grabbed the crown off his head and threw it to the floor. "I see you came prepared this time. You're smarter than I thought." He took a few steps toward Pete. His hand moved toward his pocket, but I caught his wrist.

"Ian, don't!"

He shook my hand off but left the razor in his pocket.

"Next time don't pick a fight near a gym, asshole. That's where they keep the baseball bats." Pete aimed for Ian's head and swung. Ian ducked, and one of the mannequin's faces disappeared as aluminum met plastic. It teetered, then crashed to the floor, a jumble of broken limbs.

I jumped back.

Ian slammed into Pete. *Ugh.* The bat clattered to the floor. Their arms locked around each other in some demented dance. The only sound in the room was the thudding of fist on flesh. Then Ian's fist came out of nowhere, catching Pete off guard.

"Noooooooooooooo!" I screamed, my voice drowning out the dull crunch of cartilage. Droplets of blood spurted from Pete's twisted nose and hung suspended in the air.

They broke apart. Pete stumbled backward, his eyes flooded with blood.

Ian knelt and reached for the bat. His fingers, quick and sure, latched on it. His arm swung up in a wide arc, his aim perfect.

Time slowed.

Pete's eyes darted toward me, then disappeared behind his hands.

I lunged between them.

Ian tried to pull back the blur of metal, but momentum is an uncooperative son of a bitch, and the world exploded into a million tiny, blinding lights.

The last thing I saw was Ian's beautiful, awful face.

Chapter Twenty-five

I am swimming against the current. Kicking with my strong legs. Reaching with my strong arms. Red light filters through the surface. So close I can see blurred faces. So close I can hear the distorted voices as they ping through the layers.

"Why doesn't he wake up?" Mom's voice hitches up an octave with each word.

"He's going to be fine. The doctors say this is normal."

Simon? I kick and push and claw toward the surface, but the water is soup. Thick and hot and heavy and impossible.

"Why don't we get a cup of coffee, Linda?" Dawn asks.

A door opens and closes.

I break the surface. Gravity ceases to exist, and I float, weightless, around the room. *I have wings!* I laugh as my head bumps into the ceiling. I look down. Sketch is sitting in a chair next to a hospital bed where a guy who looks like me is sleeping. Mason stands across the room, his face as gray and streaked as the rain-splattered window. I reach for Sketch. My fingers brush her hair, but she doesn't notice me.

"Can you hear me, Jonathan?" Sketch's voice pushes through the layers. She leans close to the sleeping boy's body and whispers, but I hear her words. I feel her hot breath on my ear. "You listen to me, you arrogant know-it-all. You were right. The dove lives! You hear me? The dove *lives*! So you *come back to us*!"

I fold my wings against my body and float toward the bed. I slip back into my skin, into the heaviness of my body, and the searing pain that throbs inside my head.

A groan escapes my lips.

"Jonathan?" Sketch's voice ricochets inside my skull.

"Where?" I push the word through the fire in my throat.

"You're at Methodist Hospital." Sketch looks at Mason, who sprints toward the bed.

"No." I shake my head. It shatters so I stop. "Where is... Ian?"

Sketch bites her lip. Her face is white. Mason stands next to my bed, his hands gripping the side rails. The door swings open. Heavy footsteps echo in the room. A shadow bends over me. The air floods with the scent of onions.

"Finally awake, I see. My name is Detective Payne. I need to ask you a few questions." The deep male voice slices through skin, blood, and bone. I pull away from him.

"Grace!" My eyes dart around the room, but she isn't there.

Mason shushes me. "Jonathan, it's okay. Take it easy."

I look from Sketch to Mason. "Please, please...find Grace."

"What's he talking about?" Sketch whispers to Mason, who shakes his head.

Detective Payne straightens up. "I'm sorry I can't wait for you to feel better before asking my questions, but we have two young people in juvenile lockup. A Pete Mitchell, I believe." He pulls a small notebook out of his pocket and glances at it. "And an Ian McGuire. Yes, that's right."

A voice inside my head screams and screams and screams.

"Now, I don't like locking up kids, Jonathan. I want to let one of them go, but for me to do that I need you to tell me who did this to you."

Something breaks deep inside me, and, whether I want them to or not, the memories rush back. Ian's fists pounding on Pete's face. Pete's nose twisting as blood spurts from it. Pete screaming, his hands covering his face. I can't make the images stop. My stomach heaves. I swallow the vomit down. Like an old black-and-white movie, the pictures play through my mind in slow motion. *No, Ian! Don't!* I see my lips move, though I can't hear my voice. I feel myself reaching to stop him. *No!* I cry again. He grabs the baseball bat, his eyes wild and unfocused. I see the blur of the bat coming toward me.

The detective leans over me. "I knew you'd remember. Who was it? Ian or Pete?"

Ian's eyes fly open, but the bat is moving so fast. Too fast to stop. I hear it, the sickening thud of aluminum on skull and then the movie fades to black.

❖

I open my eyes. Mom and a man in a white lab coat lean over my bed. Behind them, Dawn sits in Grace's chair next to Simon. Mason and Sketch stand by the window. The blotch in blue hovers in the corner. Where is Grace?

"Morning, sunshine! How was your nap?" A smile spreads across Simon's face.

"Jonathan! You're awake!" Mom reaches down and crushes me in a hug. "How do you feel?"

"Like I'm going to barf." Only glowing embers, I am happy to discover, remain in my throat.

Mom shoves a pan in my face and I barf.

"You have a concussion." She wipes my mouth.

"Mom." I wait until the fire retreats again, "I need to talk to Grace. Can you get her?"

"Sure, honey. Who is Grace?"

"My doctor…I think."

Mom's eyebrows scrunch together. She looks toward the man in white. "Honey, Dr. Jones is your doctor."

"But she's been taking care of me for days." My voice trails off as I see the blank look on their faces. Simon, Dawn, my mother, Mason, Sketch, the man in white, aka Dr. Jones, even the detective, they don't have a clue what I'm talking about. "She's been watching over me."

Mom puts her hand on my forehead. It is cool against my flushed skin. "Jonathan, I've been with you the whole time. I don't know of a doctor named Grace. Now, please take a breath and tell the police detective what happened to you. This is important." Mom keeps her voice slow and soft, like she's talking to an imbecile.

I look from Mom to Simon. "Make him go away. Please? I don't want to talk to him!"

"Sweetheart, you have to. You are the victim of a crime."

"No!" The fire rages. "No, I'm not. Where's Ian?" I look around the room, half expecting him to step from behind the hospital curtain like he's the wizard or something, but of course he doesn't because this isn't Oz. Even if it feels like it.

Mom turns away from me.

"He's fine," Simon whispers. "I visited him last night. I'll get word to him that you're awake."

"Thanks, Simon." My words slur and my eyelids triple in weight.

"He should rest," Dr. Jones says. Detective Payne begins to object, but Dr. Jones is tough. Almost as tough as Grace. "No, this will have to wait. I don't want him overstimulated now that he's awake. No more than one or two people visiting at a time from here on out."

"I'm staying," Mason says immediately. Mom tries to object, but her cell phone rings.

"Hello? Oh, thank God, they reached you!" She walks out the door.

Sketch leans down to kiss my forehead. Up close, I can see the streaks of black mascara that have run down her face.

"I'm okay," I tell her. Her face pinches, and more black tears flow. She follows Simon, Dawn, and the detective out the door.

Mason and I are alone in the dark room, watching the rain pummel the window. Out of the corner of my eye, I catch a flash of white light. For one split second, I see her, reflected in the window. An old woman, hands on her hips, standing inside the light. Grace. But when I turn my head, she is gone.

"Did you see that?" I ask Mason, who raises an eyebrow and looks toward the window.

"The lightning? Of course. Jonathan, are you okay?"

"I don't know." My words frighten me.

We sit there, listening to the hard rap of freezing rain as it hits the window and the constant beeps and buzzes that is life inside a hospital.

"So are you going to tell me?" Mason asks.

"Tell you what?"

"What happened in the art room?"

I roll onto my side and look at his reflection in the window. "You sure you want to know? That detective might question you."

The muscles along Mason's jaw bulge as he clenches his teeth. "Let him."

I close my eyes and tell him everything.

CHAPTER TWENTY-SIX

A phone blasts, shattering the dark quiet of my room. I blink myself awake. The window has transformed into a mirror, reflecting only the things inside my hospital room. The closet. The door. The empty chair beside my bed. The phone blasts again. I fumble for it.

"Hello?" I mumble into the receiver.

"Hey, I heard you woke up." His voice has changed since I heard it last. It is lower, slower, and more measured. "Be careful what you say, Jonathan. All the calls are recorded. Understand?"

I have no answer for that question.

"Jonathan, are you there?"

"Yeah, I'm here."

"Listen, the police are going to question you. I told them what happened. That Pete barged in on us when we were dancing. That *he* brought the baseball bat into the art room. That *he's* the one to blame. All you need to do is confirm what I've already told them. You understand?"

I hear it then, the emphasis on all the wrong words. "No one's to blame, Ian. You know it was just an acci—"

"No!" He pants into the phone. "Listen to me carefully, Jonathan! Zero weapons tolerance. Why do schools have those policies? The police aren't going stop until they've pinned the blame on somebody."

It hits me, the magnitude of the situation. "I gotta go, Ian. I'm not feeling well."

"Say it, Jonathan." His voice pitches higher and louder, and I really do feel like I am going to vomit. "Say it was Pete's fault!"

The nausea crashes in waves. "I…I'm going to throw up."

His breath comes in short pants through the receiver. "Jonathan, I love you. You know that, right?"

I can't argue with that. Partly because I am hurling into a plastic tray. I puke and I puke and I puke until everything, even the vile truth, comes up.

Later, just as a swath of orange streaks across the sky, Simon stops in. He brings me a wet washcloth from the bathroom, and I scrub off the dried bits of vomit.

"Where are Dawn and Mom?"

"In the waiting room with Detective Payne."

I can feel the muscles of my face harden. "I don't want to talk to him."

"I know, Jonathan, but you're going to have to. This thing isn't going to go away. Just tell him the truth and you'll be fine."

And suddenly, I am sick of his promises.

"I'll be fine? Really, Simon?" I shout, igniting the fire again. "Like when you said all I needed to do was believe that God's love was unconditional and I'd be fine?"

"There's a difference between God's love for us and how we sometimes treat each other. Please, Jonathan, you have to believe that." Simon reaches for my arm.

I yank it out of his grasp. "Why? Will belief change

anything? Will it make things okay with Mom? Will it get Ian and Pete out of that jail cell?"

Simon pushes the wheels of his chair. He glides away from me. "I can't promise any of those things. But I do know that God's love for you is big enough to get you through whatever the future holds."

I don't care if my throat is burning. I don't even care if my faith turns to ashes. "Is it big enough to help Ian through a trial? A conviction? Jail? Is it, Simon?"

"I see," he says softly. He should look surprised, but he doesn't. "And the answer is yes. It's big enough even for that."

Hearing him say it makes it real. I don't want to talk anymore, but Simon knows something about Ian, and every instinct I have tells me I need to know that secret. "What did he mean when he said it was official?"

He blinks. I've caught him off guard.

Simon shakes his head. "I'm sorry, Jonathan. It's not for me to say."

There have been a handful of times in my life when everything and nothing made sense all at once. The first time Pete and I touched each other, all those years ago in my bedroom when our friends slept scattered around the floor. The first time Ian kissed me. The first time I said the words *I'm gay* aloud and God didn't strike me dead. Simon refusing to answer me now.

"Then get out!" My head threatens to explode. Seriously, I can picture my brains splattered against the pale yellow wall of the hospital room. My stomach rolls again.

"Please, Jonathan, I made a promise."

"I'm sick of your promises."

Simon flinches; I plunged it deep, the sharp blade of my

anger. He turns his wheelchair with a squeak, and I watch him roll toward the door. Watch him struggle to hold it open with one hand while he pushes on the wheel with the other. His chair veers sharply and his feet bash into the door. I wince and then I remember that there are some things Simon can't feel. Can't understand. The door swooshes shut behind him, and I am alone. More alone than I have ever been before.

Of course, you're never alone in a hospital for long. There are always people wanting to take your temperature or check your blood pressure, flash lights into your eyes, dab your tears.

The door opens, and Dawn pokes her head into my room. "I can stay or I can leave. Your choice." She is one of the few people who gets that being able to choose is a damn fine thing.

"You can stay."

She sits in what I still think of as Grace's chair, but I don't mind that either. She's okay with quiet, which is one of the best things about Dawn. For once, though, I'm not.

"He's keeping something from me. Something about Ian!" I grip the call button in my hand, and I have to force myself to let go before I do something stupid like call a nurse into my room.

"You're right." She touches the delicate woven ring on her finger. She doesn't try to defend him, this man she has promised to marry.

"Why?" The betrayal I feel oozes out of me like an infection.

"He's a man of his word." And suddenly, the heat crawls up my neck and spreads across my cheeks and prickles my scalp with thousands of burning hot needles because of course she is right. Simon *would* tell me if Simon *could* tell me. Then the heat flashes. It burns through shame until it licks at my fury.

"I'm sick of easy answers, Dawn. I don't know what I believe anymore. Hell, I don't even know what's real or not."

"Yes, I heard about Grace."

I turn to look at her sharply. "Where is she?"

Dawn touches my chest, above my heart. "I'm pretty sure she's right here, Jonathan."

"Oh." I deflate. I don't even bother hiding the tears.

"Go ahead and cry," Dawn tells me. "Or yell. God knows you've earned the right to do both. But while you're crying with me or yelling at Simon or throwing bedpans at God," her hand is warm against my cool arm, "take a moment and think about the fact that He sent His *grace* to be with you in your darkest hour."

I think about that. God's grace. Sent to me. It's just a flicker. Not even a flame, but it's there. Inside me.

"I'd still like you to go to ABLAZE with me sometime," Dawn says.

I stare straight ahead and say nothing.

"Will you think about it?"

"What's the point? You heard my mom."

A cryptic smile spreads across her face. "I think you should give your mom a little more credit, Jonathan. She's quite a woman."

CHAPTER TWENTY-SEVEN

I dream of all the Ians I know.

The Ian from camp. Carrier of the straight edge razor, *It's the only way to shave,* he floats beside me in the water so inky black it's impossible to see his scars.

Wisconsin dairy farmer-to-be Ian and captive to Castro and the Hun. *I got a hard-on with your name on it,* and he sexts me his visual proof.

U of M Ian and Bovine Convention attendee. *Do you want me to stop?* he asks as he rips open a condom wrapper.

Art room Ian. *Now that's my idea of a scarlet letter,* he tells me as he stares at the blood soaking into Pete's varsity letter jacket.

Ian calling from lockup. *Say it, Jonathan. Say you know it wasn't my fault!* That Ian is the most honest of them all.

It is Monday afternoon. I have been lying in a hospital bed while Ian and Pete have been peeing into a metal toilet since Friday night. There are lots of types of lockups, but the last CT results are finally in. No brain swelling, which means I'm free to go. Mom is politely harassing the nurses to see what is taking so long. The door opens, and I have a moment of hope that quickly dissolves when Detective Payne walks in and sinks into the chair next to the bed. I am still piecing things together from when I was out cold. I remember the blotch in blue, reeking of onions and snarling into my ear. I remember Grace, her wrinkled hands perched on her hips, glaring the blotch of blue out of my room. Protecting me.

Preparing me.

For what?

Detective Payne places a digital voice recorder on the table in front of me. "I hear you're getting out. Congrats."

For this moment, that's what.

"So here's the deal." He pushes a record button. "We've got a razor with Pete's blood and Ian's fingerprints on it. We've got a baseball bat with Pete and Ian's fingerprints on it and your blood on it. We've got three kids, two in lockup pointing fingers at each other and one in a hospital refusing to talk. So I figure I only got one option: go where it all went down. So that's what I do. Talk to a few of the students. See what shakes loose. I start with Frances Mallory and Mason Kellerman. Get told to go to hell."

I pledge to plan another *Doctor Who* marathon at my house in the near future.

He continues, "Most kids are just confused. Does this mean he's gay? Did he bring that boy to the dance as a date? They have more questions than answers, but then I start talking with the guys on your soccer team."

I groan, imagining that conversation.

"Let's see." He looks at his notes. "You've been hanging around with a whole different crowd. You quit soccer to begin a gay club at school. Some of them even figure you've been doing drugs."

I start to object, but he cuts me off. "Just when I'm thinking I have the vics and the perps mixed up, one of them pulls me aside. An Ethan"—he glances at his notepad again—"Spencer. Says he's a friend of yours. Now he has a real interesting story. Care to hear it?"

I shake my head in disbelief and in answer to his question, but I know he's going to tell me anyway.

"According to Ethan, Pete Mitchell has been leading a campaign to make your life a living hell since school started. Now, that interests me. It gets me wondering why, if it was Pete who used your skull for batting practice, you'd protect him with your silence." The detective folds his hands across his stomach. "Nope, can't figure that one out at all. Way I see it, there's only one kid you'd protect. The one you walked into the school with. Ian McGuire, your boyfriend."

I hold my breath, my silence.

"Here's what I think happened. After months of denying the rumors you were gay, you brought your boyfriend to the homecoming dance. Ballsy move in a school like East Bay Christian Academy. I'll give you that, kid. You took flack for it, and Ian, who strikes me as someone with a nonexistent fuse, decided to end it. Things got out of hand. He went too far and you tried to intervene." Detective Payne's voice is quiet. Not like the blotch in blue at all. He stares into the distance, waiting for me to respond.

Tell the truth? Give the detective everything he needs to keep Ian locked up? Or lie and let Pete take the fall for this? Some people would consider that justice.

"I don't have anything to say to you." I stare at the yellow wall.

"You're refusing to answer my questions?" Detective Payne asks.

I nod, but he taps the recorder so I whisper, "That's right. I refuse."

"Then I can't help you anymore." He stands up and hits another button. Presumably stop.

"What happens now?" I look at him.

"I don't get to decide that." He walks out of the room, the faint scent of onions lingering in the air.

❖

The late afternoon light bounces off the walls and onto the stretched face of Dr. Jones.

"Here are your discharge papers." He pretends he is talking to me, but his eyes focus on my mother's face. I clear my throat and shift in my bed. "Do you have any questions?"

"Yes, how should I care for him at home?" My mother tucks the papers into her purse.

"Rest is the best medicine for Jonathan right now. He should refrain from any strenuous activity for at least a month."

No way I'm letting that opportunity go to waste. "Do you consider painting a strenuous activity?" I ask.

"Painting?" Dr. Jones turns to look at me.

"Yeah, like kitchens and living rooms and bathrooms and bedrooms and mudrooms and front entryways and hallways."

"I see. Paint fumes can trigger headaches. Also, your balance may be affected for a while, so you should stay off ladders." Dr. Jones redeems himself.

"What about school?" Mom asks and I groan.

"I'd keep him home for a few days, but there's no reason Jonathan can't go back to school after that as long as he's not vomiting or dizzy or—"

Or hallucinating hospital workers named Grace. He doesn't say it. He doesn't have to.

Redemption, it turns out, is short-lived.

So is the trip home from the hospital.

No bed in the entire history of beds has ever felt so good.

I slip under the covers of my bed in my room in my house. Butler, hissing and spitting, disagrees with me. Clearly, it has become *his bed* in *his room* in *his house* in the few short days that I have been gone. I scratch under his chin, and we settle the issue peacefully. It is a small victory, but I need as many as I can get so, I take it.

My bedroom door is wide open, left so by Mom in case I yell for her. As if. Also, she has forgotten that sound travels up as easily as it travels down.

"He's fine, Butch...we just got home." I hear Mom's voice and the back and forth creaking of Dad's recliner. I picture her in the living room, some *How to fix your gay kid* book in her lap and a cup of tea cooling on the coffee table, as she rocks back and forth and talks into her cell. "I hate to wake him up right now. The doctor says he needs to rest. Besides, you'll see him soon. What's that?...No, the detective said they had to let the boys go while they continue their investigation. Yes, both Peter Mitchell and that boy. Can you believe it, Butch? That boy brought a straight razor into our son's school, put our son in the hospital, and they let him waltz out of jail just like nothing happened? It's...What? No, he won't talk to anyone about what happened. I'm sure you'll get him to listen to reason...Me? I'm fine. Really, I am, but, please, hurry home."

His name is Ian. Not that boy. The dull ache that has taken up residence between my eyes throbs. *And it's going to take more than hauling Dad home to make me talk.* The pain presses against my skull and then releases. Ian is out of jail. Sparkles dance in front of my eyes as my lungs contract, sucking in deep gulps of air.

But Dad's coming home. Mom's called in reinforcements of her own.

Courage is endurance for one moment more.

I look at the stretch of floor where I have pushed my way up and down 100...200...300...400...500 times and beyond, shattering records, his and mine.

You won't get me to talk. I don't care what you say or do, Dad. I can out-endure you. I'd say it to his face, but he isn't home...yet.

Mom brings me a snack a few hours later. A bowl of ice cream. Two scoops. No sprinkles.

"When is he coming home?" I take the bowl and avoid her eyes.

"You heard?" The belt on her faded purple bathrobe comes untied and her robe swings open. Her collarbones jut out behind the straps of her nightgown. She wraps her robe around her thin body and sits on the edge of my bed.

"Duh." I look at the door. She strangles the cloth belt in her lap. She drops the belt, stands up, and walks away.

"He's only been gone for five months," I call after her. "Why is he coming home so early?"

She pauses at the door. "I don't want to talk about it, Jonathan. Not now."

"Then when? When it's two against one? Because you might as well tell Dad to stay in Afghanistan. I'm not helping you put Ian away." The words escape before I can think about them, but I don't care.

"Jonathan, you're upset and I'm tired. Can we talk about this later?"

"Nothing's going to be different later. You're going to have to accept the fact that you can't change who I am."

She turns her back on me, her hand grabbing for the door frame. "You think I don't know that? Honey, all I ever wanted was for you to be safe. And look what happened." Her shoulders swell and retreat, swell and retreat, and I hear the tears thick in her voice. "I talked with Simon and Dawn while you were in the hospital. Their views are, well, I don't know what to think. But I canceled the appointment at Deliverance Clinic until I understand this issue more. I'm doing the very best that I can, Jonathan. I hope you believe that."

My head spins. I don't know what to think or believe. "Then why is Dad coming home?"

Breath leaks from her like she's been punctured. "Not everything is about you, Jonathan. That's a fact you need to accept." She lets go of the door frame and walks out of my room, leaving the door cracked open between us just in case.

Ian? I text the minute I hear her footsteps on the stairway. *Are you okay?* But that's not quite the right question so I send another message. *Are we okay?* I ask and lay down on my bed to wait for his reply.

Hours later, still waiting, I fall asleep with my cell phone on my pillow.

CHAPTER TWENTY-EIGHT

I stand outside Young at Art on Wednesday night with two conflicting agendas.

First, I want to check out One Heart's youth group. A church where I can be myself, my *whole* self, and be accepted? Sounds like one of Sketch's sci-fi shows.

Second, I want answers, and I am prepared to push. The door. Simon. Dawn. The fact that they trust me. I start with the door, but the tinkling bell sounds so friendly, I almost turn around and leave. Then I catch sight of the forest mural and the shimmering wall of glass that is, somehow, Spirit Lake. The memories return, and I have to know the rest of the story.

"Hello?" My voice echoes in the large room. She did say Wednesday, didn't she? "Simon? Dawn?"

I hear the bark before I see the blur of white. Bear, impossibly bigger than the last time I saw him, bounds at me. I steel myself for the inevitable assault.

"Bear, sit!" Dawn's voice comes from the doorway that leads to the kitchen and, shocker of all shockers, he does. She beams. "Make sure you remind Simon that he called obedience classes a waste of money, will you?"

"You got it." I pat Bear's head and whisper *good boy*. "Where is Simon?"

"Meeting with the Department of Child Welfare to see how we can help Ian." Dawn looks at her watch. "You're early. ABLAZE doesn't start until seven p.m."

"Yeah, I know, but I wanted to talk to him about what happened in the hospital."

"He forgives you, Jonathan. You know that. How about a cup of tea?"

I follow Dawn into the kitchen. I do not point out that I haven't asked for Simon's forgiveness.

"I'm so glad you talked your mom into letting you go tonight. What an answer to prayer!"

The truth is, going to ABLAZE was Mom's idea, but truth has little to do with today's mission. "So Ian called me." I sit at the small table and watch Dawn fuss with a teapot. Technically, it's the truth if you count the call in the hospital. I've sent him maybe ten more texts since I heard he was released from jail. So far, no response from Ian. Either Matilda the Hun and Fidel Castro have nixed his phone privileges or… well, I don't like to think about the other possible reason for Ian's silence.

He blames me for what happened.

"How's he doing?" Dawn takes down a canister from a cupboard and spoons something into a mug. Steam spouts from the kettle.

"Not so hot, Dawn. He's hoping his attorney can make a case based on, you know, what happened to him." This is a risk, but it's a calculated one.

Out of the corner of my eye, I see her turn and look at me. "So he finally told you? I'm so glad. It was tearing Simon up having to keep this from you, but Ian made him promise."

I get real interested in a tree outside real fast. Like I start counting bare branch after bare branch and crap like that. The secret to lying, I've learned, is sticking as close to the truth as possible. "I still don't get why he didn't want me to know."

One…two…three…I hold my breath and wait.

"Don't take it personally, Jonathan. What Ian's parents did hurt him deeply. I'm sure he's been wrestling with all sorts of emotions. Anger, shame, even envy for the life you have. Your mom and dad might not be perfect, but they'd never relinquish their parental rights," Dawn says, and I feel the click, deep inside, as the pieces slide into place. *Official,* he'd said.

"No, you're right. They wouldn't ever do that to me." I stare at the tree until I'm sure it will burst into flame. "What's going to happen to him now?"

"Worst case scenario? The state decides to press charges. It's a serious thing, bringing a weapon into the school and hurting students. Best case? The investigation is dropped and Ian will continue to live with the Castells. I know it's not ideal, but he doesn't have many options as a ward of the state." The kettle begins to wail. Softly at first, but rising until I want to scream too.

Ward of the state. As in the final cutting of the ties that should bind. "I forgot to ask him when they filed the paperwork." The words come so easily. So effortlessly.

Dawn pours the steaming water into the mug. The scent of orange and cloves fills the air. "I think he got the document from the courts about a month ago. He must have been devastated."

Around the time he wanted us to run away together. When he called my life perfect. Of course! I am an idiot.

"He was." I turn away from the window. Dawn places the mug of tea in front of me, and I lift it to my face, the steam masking the moisture from my eyes. "It changed him."

"How could it not? To know that the people who should love you the most can reject you? It would change anyone."

"Mom says I might have to meet with Detective Payne again. Give a statement." My throat ignites again. I blink away the tears. "I won't help him hurt Ian, Dawn!"

She puts her arm around me. "Have you thought that telling the truth might actually help Ian?"

I pull away. "You're nuts."

She shakes her head. "No, I'm not. Think about it. You walked away from that fight for months! But he wasn't able to. This pain he carries is an open, bleeding wound. Maybe this is the intervention Ian needs. Before it's too late for him. Who knows? God works in miraculous ways, Jonathan."

I begin to tell Dawn that Ian might view things just a titch different, when she glances at her watch and yelps. "You know what else will be a miracle?"

"What?"

"You and me getting to the church on time!" She jumps up, tells Bear to behave himself, and grabs her jacket off the hook by the kitchen door.

The clock in Dawn's car reads 7:03 when we pull into One Heart's parking lot. Three minutes late. Not bad, though my hand appears to be glued to the *oh crap* handle in her car. Dawn sprints up the steps, flings open the door, and we burst into the circular church foyer. Dawn strides toward what I assume is the meeting room. I don't move, except to slow swivel and take it all in.

You are welcome here!

God loves you JUST AS YOU ARE!

Enter in peace and know that you are God's beloved!

The banners stream down from the ceiling. One—two—three—seven of them, each one a different color. A rainbow of love and acceptance. My head spins. The result of my head injury? Maybe. Maybe not.

There is a—how is this possible?—a tree growing in the middle of the foyer!

Its roots plunge into the ground, far beneath the slate floor. Its branches, filled with small round fruit, spread out above my head.

"Can I help you?" a woman speaks behind me. Not Dawn.

I turn and look into gray eyes.

"There's a tree in your church," I say, realizing how dumb that sounds moments after I say it.

She chuckles. "Good observation. Care to know why?" the tall, thin woman asks me. Ratty jeans. Sandals. A plain white shirt with her sleeves rolled up above her elbows. Short silver hair. She is youthful if not young.

"Sure," I say.

She kneels and places her hand on the patch of dirt that bridges between the flooring and the tree. "You've seen pictures of the dove carrying an olive branch, right?"

I nod, remembering the stained glass windows at Redeemer.

"But have you ever seen an olive tree? Look at it. Look closely." She nods toward the base of the tree.

I look. Is it one tree or many? The trunk is a mass of individual branches that have risen out of the ground and entwined together.

"This is how the family of Christ should be. As He taught us to be. Made stronger as we weave our lives together. Rooted in our love of God. Peace, the fruit of our fellowship, freely available to everyone, and shelter"—she raises her hands, palms smudged with dirt, toward the ceiling—"given to all who are in need." She smiles at me. "And you, if I am not mistaken, are Dawn's friend Jonathan Cooper. Welcome to One Heart Church. I've been praying for you."

I'm used to people praying for me. Friends. Family. Pastor Jim. But it startles me to hear these words from a stranger kneeling at the foot of an olive tree.

"You don't know me." There I go again, stating the obvious.

"I didn't realize that was a criteria for prayer." She stands and holds out a dirty hand. "But it's easily remedied. My name is Jane. I'm the pastor here. I will be the first, but certainly not the last, to tell you that you are welcome at this church. Just as you are."

I shake her hand. Dirt flecks and all. "Nice to meet you." I want to say more. Maybe something like *Are you for real, lady?* but my throat tightens, and I'm not sure I can trust my voice.

Dawn pokes her head out of the meeting room. "There you are, Jonathan! We're waiting on you!"

I say good-bye to Pastor Jane and quickstep it toward Dawn.

There are no banners inside the meeting room. Just a different kind of rainbow. A girl with blue-black hair and sculpted cheekbones, a younger version of Dawn. I spot an ear bud in her left ear and the tapping of her orange high-top tennis shoes. A guy in a multicolored flowing shirt, not a style I'm used to, but he smiles at me, his teeth startlingly white against the dark ebony of his skin. I look around the circle at the ten or so other kids who are part of ABLAZE, each one unafraid to shine, and feel about as dull as a glass of milk.

I pick the open chair next to Dawn. I am expecting the curious glances. Just not the greetings of *Hi, Jonathan!*

Welcome! When it's time for introductions, I plan on only telling them my name, but suddenly, I am talking about how cool it is that there is a tree growing inside their church and then, don't ask me why, I tell them about the willow tree at Spirit Lake Bible Camp and how I used to sit inside its long branches when I was a kid and homesick and how a storm hit last summer and now the only thing left of my willow tree is a pile of kindling. And when I finish rambling, the flush of the impromptu confession spreading across my face, I notice that Dawn isn't the only one blinking away tears.

I am too.

I think about the olive tree all the way home and later that night when I'm soaking in the bathtub, the one place where privacy is guaranteed. I think about the branches woven together as I sit in the tub, watching it fill with water and bubbles as Butler hisses outside the closed bathroom door. He doesn't even like the sound of running water. I am picturing Pastor Jane, her palms flecked with dirt and pointed toward heaven, when my phone rings. I pick it up, praying I don't drop it in the tub. It's Mason.

"I require a status update. How are you?"

"Confused, thank you." Mason is a human lie detector, so I don't even bother.

"What's that sound?"

"A running faucet. Why?"

"No reason. You're not in the middle of drowning yourself in the bathtub, are you?"

"Yes and no. Did you call for any particular reason or just to annoy me?"

"I called to remind you about *The Scarlet Letter* essay." He sounds relieved, or maybe irritated. Either seems likely. "It's due tomorrow."

"Wonderful." So much for a relaxing bath. I yank the drain out. The tub gives a monster belch, fitting in a room dedicated to *The Sounds of Nature*.

"So you're coming back to school tomorrow?"

"Tragically, yes."

"Do you know what you're writing about yet?"

"Not a clue."

"Gilchrist would probably give you an extension. I mean, you've been *in the hospital*." He says this like I was on life support. "And then there is *the thing with Ian*."

"Good-bye, Mason." I push the end call button with a sudsy finger, telling myself it's not technically hanging up on a person if I say good-bye.

It strikes me, as I watch the liquid tornado swirl down the drain, that Mason is right. Gilchrist would give me an extension, but I'm sick of delaying the inevitable. I dry off and tell Mom good night as I walk past the living room. She asks me what I thought of ABLAZE, but I put on my deaf ears and climb the stairs to my room where I open a Word document on my computer.

The accused: Hester Prynne

The real crime: Obstruction of Justice

by Jonathan Cooper

American lit, second period.

The extension is tempting as I look at the blinking cursor on the page, but I push ahead.

Hester Prynne slept with another man while she was married. She conceived a child by him. She was, therefore, guilty of adultery. But that was not the real crime for which she was punished. Hester Prynne refused to identify of the baby's father, despite being asked repeatedly by officials of the court. Her real crime was obstruction of justice, and it was this offense that caused the people of Salem to turn their backs on her.

I pause and remember. Mom brushing tears from her eyes, pleading with me to tell her what happened in the art room. Detective Payne's shoulders sagging as he presses the stop button on the recording machine. Dawn. *Maybe this is the intervention Ian needs.*

It surfaces. The doubt. The fear. The truth.

But then Hester stands beside me, whispering that sometimes the only way to serve justice is by keeping silent.

My fingers glide over my keyboard. There is no stopping them.

Hester Prynne obstructed justice. Not because she disrespected the law. Not because she held out hope that someday she could be with the man she loved. No, she knew they would never allow that. My hands shook. *Hester Prynne stayed silent because it was the only way she could protect the man she loved.*

It shudders into focus.

The dazzling discovery of love.

The despair when that dream is crushed.

Something breaks inside me and the words pour like blood from a head wound all over the page, splashing and messy and uncontainable. And hours later, I fall into bed, emptied, but with an essay to give Gilchrist in the morning.

If I am right, it does not completely suck.

CHAPTER TWENTY-NINE

"Okay, everyone. How about a hypothetical question?" Sketch asks during lunch on Thursday, my first day back to school. We have commandeered a table large enough to hold fifteen people. Sketch, Mason, and me, of course. But also Nick, Jessica and her girlfriend, the chess club, the guys in the sci-fi T-shirts, and Ethan. Yes, Ethan. He has abandoned the table with the view of the lake to sit with us.

"Fire away." I take a bite of spaghetti.

"The Doctor shows up with the TARDIS. Where do you ask him to take you and why?"

It's a great question. An intriguing question. A brilliant question. "Jonathan, you start." It's also a total ruse to shield me from all the other questions our new crowd is dying to ask me.

I think about it for a few seconds. "Salem, Massachusetts, eighteen something."

Mason puts down his fork and raises an eyebrow. "Why would you want to talk to Nathanial Hawthorne?"

"Because I'm becoming more and more bewildered the longer I try to wear two faces."

Mason smiles. Ethan stares at the puckered scar on my head. "Are you sure you're ready to be back at school?"

I try to explain about Reverend Dimmesdale and how he pretended to be someone he wasn't and hated himself in the end. I try to do justice to Hester Prynne and how she never betrayed herself or the man she loved.

I fail.

"Wait? You want to travel in time to talk to some dead guy about a musty old book?" Ethan sneaks another glance at my scar.

"It's *The Scarlet Letter*," Mason explains. "We studied it in American lit. If I had to guess I'd say Jonathan is finally ready to tell us something."

They stare at me, waiting. All of them.

I haven't planned this, but if I had I sure as hell wouldn't have picked the middle of a crowded cafeteria. But I guess coming out is a lot like falling in love, only you're falling in love with yourself. The minute you realize it, you need to say the words.

"I'm gay," I say and wait for their shocked and indignant responses.

Nick takes a sip of milk. Jessica takes a bite of spaghetti. Mason takes a long look at me and smiles. And Sketch? Well, she takes my hand and squeezes.

"I'm sorry I didn't tell you guys earlier."

"Nothing to be sorry about, dude," Ethan says, and then it descends. The awkwardness that follows all confessions.

Pete walks into the cafeteria carrying a tray, stealing the focus from me. Who would have thought, after all we'd been through, that I could still feel gratitude to Pete Mitchell? He takes a few steps toward the table where Brandon, Austin, and Zack are sitting, stops, and looks around. It's his first day back too.

"So, Jonathan." Mason notices me staring at Pete and tries to snap me out of it. "It dawns on me that while I've heard you talk about *Two Men Dancing* a million times, I've never actually seen the picture in person. I'm feeling left out." He looks around the table. "Anyone want to go to the Walker after school today?"

Ethan has winter traveling soccer tryouts. Nick and the rest of the chess team have, well, the chess team. Jessica has band practice. The nos stack up until Mason looks from Sketch to me.

"I can't," she says. "I promised Simon I'd help him with his new class. Toddlers and Pottery Training. Tell me it's not going to be as bad as I think it is!"

I laugh. Mostly because the name is one hundred percent Simon-grade brilliance, but also at the thought of Sketch chasing around a classroom full of muddy two-year-olds. "Maybe we should help her?"

Mason shoots a withering look at me. "Absolutely not. These slacks came from Nordstrom." He shudders, and I don't even try to hide my eye-rolling. "You and I are going to the Walker. No toddlers and no arguments."

"Fine. You two leave me alone to chase after slippery barbarians." Sketch pouts.

Pete walks away from the table by the lake and sits at a small table in the corner by himself. His head hangs, but not so low that I can't see his eyes surrounded by a sea of purple.

I detangle my legs from the cafeteria table.

"Where are you going?" Sketch asks me.

"Be right back." I look toward Pete.

"Aw, *hell no!*" Mason hisses.

Sketch, brows furrowed, says nothing. I ignore them both and walk across the cafeteria. The heat from a thousand eyes burns into me. Silence descends. I stop a few feet away from his table, uncertain what to say or do. He senses me and turns around. I look into the face of my frenemy. Pete, but not Pete.

His nose is confused. It doesn't know which way to go. Left. Right. Any direction but straight on seems to work. Up close, I can see the purple sea that surrounds his eyes better. Like colors on an oil painting, purple blends into yellow and flecks of dark mottled red. I hurt just looking at him.

Pete stares at me, his blue irises cold.

"Hey," I say and shift my weight.

"So I suppose you think I should thank you for keeping your mouth shut?"

"I didn't do it for you."

"Then what do you want?" He sits up a little, winces and contracts his body like he's touched a hot surface.

His wounds run deep. I know how he feels.

"Just wanted to see how you are." I look around the cafeteria. At the staring faces, the gaping mouths, at Brandon and Zack and Austin who are sitting by the window, at Mason who is shaking his head, at Sketch and Ethan who are trying to pick a facial expression. I stare back at them, all of them, until one by one they look away.

"How are you?" I ask, sitting down. Most of the time, in polite society, people answer this question with *fine*. Pete and I are past being polite.

"Cashing a payback check." He curls his lip into a half-smile, half-sneer. "That must get your rocks off."

"It doesn't," I say. "Not at all."

We sit there in the crowded, silent cafeteria. Two friends who once were kids, trying to make sense of the incomprehensible. Two enemies who, just under the surface, are only afraid of the same thing. Neither of us has the first clue what to say.

I reach for something normal. "You finish your essay?"

"Barely, I wrote about how the ending seemed sorta sappy with the three of them riding off together."

It sinks in.

"The three of them? Pete, tell me you didn't just watch the movie?"

He smirks, and I recognize the mask. "That was some sweet nipple action."

I break it to him as gently as I can. "Dimmesdale died at the end of the novel. Hester and Pearl left together. Just the two of them."

It doesn't seem possible, but Pete reaches new levels of pathetic.

"I am so fucked." He runs his fingers through his hair, winces, and hangs his head.

"Maybe Gilchrist will let you rewrite it?" I offer.

Pete's shoulders drop an inch as he exhales. "I'm not talking about Gilchrist! Everyone is talking about what Ian said. About me. And how I…reacted…when he grabbed me."

Finally!

"It's just gossip, Pete. You can ride it out."

"And in the meantime?"

"In the meantime"—I stand up—"you can sit with us. Anytime you want." There will be hell to pay with Mason if Pete ever takes me up on my offer. I extend it anyway.

"Like that would make the rumors go away faster." He has a point. "I might as well show up at one of your damn meetings."

"You'd be welcome there. Anytime."

Pete says nothing. He lifts his sandwich to his mouth, flinches, and touches the place where his lip is split. The conversation has reached its natural conclusion.

But it's not over. Not until I say what I came over here to say. "Just because we once—" Pete glances around the cafeteria and looks at me, scowling. I rush on before he can throw a punch or I can chicken out. "Look, we were kids. It didn't mean anything. Just because I'm gay doesn't mean you are, and I wanted you to know," I drop my voice to the softest of whispers, "I'll never tell anyone about what happened between us. I swear to God."

No one is more surprised than I am to find it's an oath that still means something to me.

"Yeah, whatever. Later, Coop."

"Okay, Pete. I guess I'll see you around."

CHAPTER THIRTY

It is a quiet ride to the Walker after school. Even Sketch is silent until we pull up to Young at Art where she finally finds her voice. It must be the proximity to Simon. Stranger things have happened.

"Don't give him shit, Mason. He did the right thing."

Mason's jaw drops, and for a minute, I think he's going to argue about it, but Sketch coats her voice in steel. "And don't you take any shit from him, Jonathan." She slips out of the car and heads toward the art studio.

"She's right." I try to defrost the iciness that is coming off Mason like an arctic front. "It's just like what happened to me. People spreading rumors, not caring who it hurts."

"It's nothing like what happened to you. You would never have treated someone the way Pete treated you."

I stop talking and watch him maneuver the roads into downtown Minneapolis. We walk past the ginormous cherry on the ginormous spoon and into the Walker, where a familiar voice breaks the silence.

"Well, hello, Jonathan! Where's my Francie?" Sketch's grandmother greets us.

"She's helping Simon with a class at Young at Art. It's a new art studio in Uptown."

"That's my Francie! A real artist. Ray, did you hear that? My Francie is working at an art studio!"

"What's that about Francie?" Ray asks as he hands me two orange tabs that read *Walker.* I clip one to my shirt pocket and give Mason the other.

"Aren't you going to introduce your new friend?" Enid wags a finger at me.

"I'm sorry. Mason, this is Enid, Sketch's grandmother."

"Why, it's a real pleasure to meet you." She places her wrinkled, liver-spotted hand on Mason's. Pat. Pat. She smiles a yellow-toothed grin at him. "Ray, say hello to Jonathan's friend, Mason."

"What's that?"

"I said *say hello to Jonathan's friend,* you deaf old fool."

I shoot a sideways glance at Mason and wink because it really is too funny and I have forgotten that he's mad at me, but Enid spots me.

"Now, Jonathan, don't you start flirting with me. I have my pacemaker to think of!" She smirks.

We say good-bye to Enid and Ray and walk past the row of windows shaped like trapezoids and parallelograms, the sound of our footsteps echoing throughout the long white corridor of gleaming marble. We burst into laughter when we are far enough away to not be overheard.

"That explains a whole lot about Sketch," Mason says, and things are normal, if unresolved, between us. We turn the corner into the gallery, and I can't stop my eyes from wandering toward his face as we draw nearer to the small black-and-white photograph.

"Here it is," I say when we stand in front of it. "*Two Men Dancing* by Robert Mapplethorpe."

The only sound is my lungs sucking air in and pushing it out. Beside me, Mason has stopped breathing.

"God, that's…"

"Impossible, right?" I finish his sentence.

"I was going to say inspiring. Nothing about that picture is impossible."

"You're wrong."

"Why?" Mason's espresso eyes are dialed to high alert. He sees everything. "Because of what happened?"

"Yeah, maybe."

"Listen, you had one dance and it didn't go so great, but that doesn't mean you quit dancing for good." Mason stands in front of the Mapplethorpe and holds his arms out, which is ridiculous.

Really it is. I mean, who does that? In the middle of an art gallery with *people* milling around? With Enid and old deaf Ray just down the hallway? With Robert Mapplethorpe and his two dancing men looking on? Who stands there with his arms outstretched, expecting me to just…

I turn away and look toward the exit. "Are you hungry?" I ask.

"Ravenous." His voice lights something deep in my belly.

We find a booth in Gather, the restaurant at the Walker, and Mason orders an appetizer of French fries with truffle aioli. I ask him what an aioli is. He laughs and tells me to shut up and eat it, so I do. He sips a non-alcoholic drink of cucumber, lime, mint, lemonade, and ginger ale, which sounds gross but tastes delicious. I drink my boring old Coke and listen to him ramble on about the influence of modern art on fashion design. I tell him about One Heart and Pastor Jane and the olive tree in the circular foyer and how it must be too good to be true.

Mason looks up at me over his no-jito and, after an awkward pause that feels like forever, tells me that real love always feels too good to be true.

The sky grows dark, and I know the proverbial shit is about to hit the proverbial fan at home. Mason and I say good-bye to Enid and Ray. We promise we'll come back and bring Francie with us next time. We walk the block and a half to his car and drive home, Mason blasting "Mannish Boy" by Muddy Waters the whole way.

He turns into my driveway. The curtains in the front window open and Mom stands there, the light from behind turning her into a silhouette, as she peers into the night, watching over me. Spying on me? No, just trying to keep me safe.

"So that was, uh, fun," he says.

"Yeah, it was."

"As much fun as when you and Sketch took the TARDIS?" Mason's question hangs in the car like our foggy breath.

"Maybe more."

He grins in the dark. "You know where I would have gone if the Doctor showed up with his TARDIS?"

"Where?" It's been a weird day. Anything is possible.

"Not far. Not even that long ago. Just to last summer. To the opening day at a certain camp. There's someone I'd like to get to know before things get complicated."

"Mason…I…" I sit there and stammer like an idiot.

"But I guess there's no point in going back in time. The only thing that matters is what's happening today. And what could happen tomorrow." He peers at me through the darkness, his face illuminated by the light from his dashboard.

I know what he wants. I also know I'm not ready.

I say nothing.

Mason turns in the seat and stares out his window. "Okay, then. I'll wait."

Outside, the wind whips the bare branches of the trees. Tiny flakes of snow, the first of the new season, swirl in the light from the street lamp. A flake lands on Mason's windshield and melts.

"I should go," I say while I still can.

CHAPTER THIRTY-ONE

Two weeks later, I am sitting in the living room on a Saturday morning, waiting for Mom.

"Jonathan, would you warm up the car?" she calls from the bathroom, where she has been fussing with her hair for thirty minutes. I throw on a jacket and schlep through the foot-high snow to the garage and Dad's car.

I slip in the key and crank the heat, another step closer to the inevitable, still thinking about Sketch's hypothetical question.

The Doctor shows up with the TARDIS. Where do you go?

"Hmm, I think Boston, Massachusetts, today." I'm not going to lie; talking to myself in an idling car isn't my finest moment.

Mom opens the passenger door and slides in next to me, the thick scent of Chanel No. 5 swirling around her, a scarf wrapped around her head. "Ready to go pick him up?"

"Sure." I drive away from our house and out of our neighborhood, but in my mind I am inside the TARDIS, hurtling toward a different man. One who is too young to be dying. It's not fair.

Hello, Mr. Mapplethorpe, I would say, photographer

to photographer, as I light his cigarette and fluff his pillow. When he is comfortable, I'd bend close to him and whisper my question in his ear and he would smile.

He might even reach up with a frail hand, pat my face, and nod.

"Of course you will," he'd say and then his words would dissolve into a fit of coughing and I'd tiptoe out of the room, grateful for everything he's given me.

I maneuver the car onto the exit for the international airport where planes, *real planes,* exist, though they feel less real to me than Sketch's TARDIS.

I park the car. Mom adjusts her scarf, pinches her cheeks, and applies another layer of lipstick. Her happiness is a tangible thing, and I am glad for her.

"How do I look?"

"Beautiful," I tell her the truth, which makes her smile.

We find seats in the waiting area of the airport. Mom watches the planes take off and land while I think about the fact that one of them is bringing Dad home.

Mom runs her hand over my buzz cut. "Your father will be so pleased," she says about my new haircut, compliments of the hospital staff, and she's right. Dad is coming home to the crew cut–wearing son he's always wanted.

I bend over, let my head fall into my hands, and close my eyes.

"Are you all right, honey?" she asks, and I almost tell her, but I know now that while I can be truthful and I can be kind, sometimes I can't be both.

"Of course," I say.

Will I ever hear from Ian again?

What will Dad say when he walks through that airport gate?

Will this ache inside me ever go away?

I hear it then, the music I forgot along the journey. It swells until it drowns out the overhead announcements and the sounds of busy travelers rushing along, their luggage wheels squeaking behind them.

Mom rests her hand on my back.

She says nothing, but the warmth of her touch is enough.

Just like it is enough to wear this one face I've been given. To believe that God sent His grace to watch over me in my darkest hour. And to know that someday, maybe not today, but someday, I'll even dance again.

About the Author

Minnesota writer Juliann Rich spent her childhood in search of the perfect climbing tree. The taller the better! A branch thirty feet off the ground and surrounded by leaves, caterpillars, birds, and squirrels was a good perch for a young girl to find herself. Seeking truth in nature and finding a unique point of view remain crucial elements in her life as well as her writing.

Juliann is a PFLAG mom who can be found walking Pride parades with her son. She is also the daughter of evangelical Christian parents. As such she has been caught in the crossfire of the most heated topic to challenge our society and our churches today. She is drawn to stories that shed light on the conflicts that arise when sexual orientation, spirituality, family dynamics and peer relationships collide. You can read more about her journey as an author and as an affirming mom on her website, www.juliannrich.com and her blog, www.therainbowtreeblog.com.

Juliann is the author of two affirmative young adult novels: *Caught in the Crossfire* and *Searching for Grace*. She is the 2014 recipient of the Emerging Writer Award from The Saints and Sinners Literary Festival and lives with her husband and their two dogs, Mr. Sherlock Holmes and Ms. Bella Moriarty, in the beautiful Minnesota River Valley.

Soliloquy Titles From Bold Strokes Books

Searching for Grace by Juliann Rich. First it's a rumor. Then it's a fact. And then it's on. (978-1-62639-196-3)

Dark Tide by Greg Herren. A summer working as a lifeguard at a hotel on the Gulf Coast seems like a dream job…until Ricky Hackworth realizes the town is shielding some very dark—and deadly—secrets. (978-1-62639-197-0)

Everything Changes by Samantha Hale. Raven Walker's world is turned upside down the moment Morgan O'Shea walks into her life. (978-1-62639-303-5)

Fifty Yards and Holding by David Matthew-Barnes. The discovery of a secret relationship between Riley Brewer, the star of the high school baseball team, and Victor Alvarez, the leader of a violent street gang, escalates into a preventable tragedy. (978-1-62639-081-2)

Tristant and Elijah by Jennifer Lavoie. After Elijah finds a scandalous letter belonging to Tristant's great-uncle, the boys set out to discover the secret Uncle Glenn kept hidden his entire life and end up discovering who they are in the process. (978-1-62639-075-1)

Caught in the Crossfire by Juliann Rich. Two boys at Bible camp; one forbidden love. (978-1-62639-070-6)

Frenemy of the People by Nora Olsen. Clarissa and Lexie have despised each other for as long as they can remember, but when they both find themselves helping an unlikely contender for homecoming queen, they are catapulted into an unexpected romance. (978-1-62639-063-8)

The Balance by Neal Wooten. Love and survival come together in the distant future as Piri and Niko faceoff against the worst factions of mankind's evolution. (978-1-62639-055-3)

The Unwanted by Jeffrey Ricker. Jamie Thomas is plunged into danger when he discovers his mother is an Amazon who needs his help to save the tribe from a vengeful god. (978-1-62639-048-5)

Because of Her by KE Payne. When Tabby Morton is forced to move to London, she's convinced her life will never be the same again. But the beautiful and intriguing Eden Palmer is about to show her that this time, change is most definitely for the better. (978-1-62639-049-2)

The Seventh Pleiade by Andrew J. Peters. When Atlantis is besieged by violent storms, tremors, and a barbarian army, it will be up to a young gay prince to find a way for the kingdom's survival. (978-1-60282-960-2)

Asher's Fault by Elizabeth Wheeler. Fourteen-year-old Asher Price sees the world in black and white, much like the photos he takes, but when his little brother drowns at the same moment Asher experiences his first same-sex kiss, he can no longer hide behind the lens of his camera and eventually discovers he isn't the only one with a secret. (978-1-60282-982-4)

Meeting Chance by Jennifer Lavoie. When man's best friend turns on Aaron Cassidy, the teen keeps his distance until fate puts Chance in his hands. (978-1-60282-952-7)

Lake Thirteen by Greg Herren. A visit to an old cemetery seems like fun to a group of five teenagers, who soon learn that sometimes it's best to leave old ghosts alone. (978-1-60282-894-0)